# The King's Fifth

# The King's Fifth

SCOTT O'DELL

*Decorations and Maps by Samuel Bryant*

HOUGHTON MIFFLIN COMPANY BOSTON

LIBRARY OF CONGRESS CATALOG CARD NUMBER AC 66-10726

ISBN: 0-395-06963-7
ISBN-13: 978-0-395-06963-9

PRINTED IN THE U.S.A.

VB                   24 25 26 27 28 29 30

For

LUCE

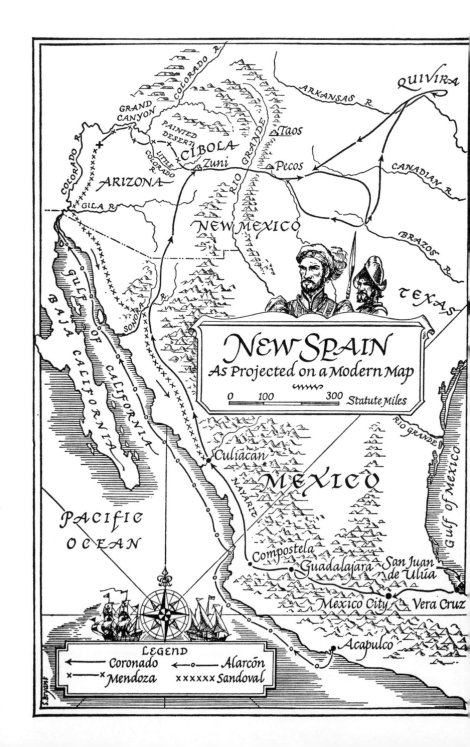

*The Fortress of San Juan de Ulúa*
*Vera Cruz, in New Spain*
*The twenty-third day of September*
*The year of our Lord's birth, 1541*

IT IS DARK NIGHT on the sea but dusk within my cell. The jailer has gone. He has left six fat candles and a bowl of garbanzos that swim in yellow oil.

I am a fortunate young man. At least this is what the jailer said just before he closed the iron door and left me alone.

He stands in the doorway and says under his breath, "Garbanzos, a slice of mutton, the best oil from Úbeda! Who ever has heard of such fine fare in His Majesty's prison? And do not forget the candles stolen from the chapel, for which I could be tossed into prison myself. Worse, mayhap."

He pauses to draw a long finger across his throat.

"Remember these favors," he says, "when you return to the land of the Seven Cities. Remember them also if by chance you do not return. Remember, Estéban de Sandoval, that I risk my life in your behalf!"

He leans toward me. His shadow fills the cell.

"I have *maravedis*, a few cents," I answer, "to pay for your kindness."

"Kindness!" He grinds the word between his teeth.

**1**

During his life he must have ground many words for his teeth are worn close. "I do not risk my neck from kindness, which is a luxury of the rich. Or for a few ducats, either. Let us be clear about this matter."

He closes the iron door and takes one long step toward me.

"I have seen the charge brought against you by the Royal Audiencia," he says. "Furthermore, I deem you guilty of that charge. But guilty or not, I ask a share of the gold you have hidden in Cíbola. The King demands his fifth. A fifth I likewise demand. For I do more than he and at dire peril to my life."

His words take me aback. "If I am found guilty," I say evasively, "then I shall never return to Cíbola."

"It is not necessary that you return. You are a maker of maps. A good one, it is said. Therefore you will draw me a map, truthful in all details, by which I can find my way to this secret place." His voice falls to a whisper. "How much gold is hidden there? Tell me, is it enough to fill the hold of a large galleon?"

"I do not know," I answer, being truthful and at the same time untruthful.

"Enough, perhaps, to fill a small galleon?"

I am silent. Two fingers thrust toward me, sudden as a snake, and nip my arm.

"You may have heard the name Quentín de Cardoza," the jailer says, "An excellent gentleman, in any event, and innocent as a new-born babe. Yet four years he spent in San Juan de Ulúa, in this very cell. And died in this cell before his trial came to an end. You also may spend four

2

years here, or five, or even more. Trials of the Royal Audiencia consume time, as dropping water consumes stone. These trials have two equal parts. One part takes place in the chambers above, before the judges. The other part takes place here below, under my watchful eye."

He tightens his grip on my arm and moves his face so close to mine that I can see the bristles on his chin.

"Remember, *señor*, that what I do for you I do not for a handful of *maravedis*. Neither for money nor from kindness. I do it only because of a chart, limned with patience and skill, which you will make for me."

"It is a crime," I answer, still being evasive, "to draw a map without permission of the Council of the Indies."

He loosens his grip upon my arm. "The Council," he says, "resides in Spain, thousands of leagues away."

"So also does the King who accuses me of theft," I boldly say.

"Yes, but do not forget that the King's loyal servant, Don Felipe de Soto y Ríos, does not reside in Spain. He stands here before you, a man with one eye which never sleeps."

Don Felipe steps back and squares his shoulders. He is tall, with a long, thin forehead and a jaw like a cudgel. He says nothing more. Softly, too softly, he closes the door and slides the iron bolt. His footsteps fade away into the depths of the fortress.

Don Felipe de Soto y Ríos! The name stirs in my memory. Is he the one who years ago marched with bloody Guzmán, who slaughtered hundreds of Tarascans and

3

dragged their king through the village streets tied to the tail of a horse?

I cannot say for certain. It does not matter. Whoever he is he has done much for me during my six days in San Juan de Ulúa. My cell is the largest in the prison, three strides one way, four strides the other. He has given me the bench I write upon, candles, paper, an inkbowl and two sharp quills.

I know now why he has given me these things. Still, I have them. In return, because I must, I shall draw him a map of Cíbola, proper in scale, deserts and mountains and rivers set down, also windroses and a Lullian nocturnal. As for the treasure which he covets, who knows where it lies? Even I who secreted it, do I know? Could I ever find it again?

Don Felipe I will not see until dawn. I can give my thoughts to the trial that begins in two days, curiously enough on my seventeenth birthday. I will put down everything as I remember it. And write carefully from the beginning, each night while the trial lasts.

Yes, I shall put down everything, just as I remember it.

I am a maker of maps and not a scrivener, yet I shall do my best. By this means, I may find the answer to all that puzzles me. God willing, I shall find my way through the labyrinth which leads to the lair of the minotaur. This should help me in the trial I face before the Royal Audiencia, for if I do not clearly know what I did or why it was done, how can I ask others to know?

I am now ready to begin. The night stretches before me. It is quiet in my cell except for the sound of water

4

dripping somewhere and the lap of waves against the fortress walls. The candle sheds a good light. Some say that in the darkness one candle can shine like the sun.

And yet where is the beginning? What first step shall I take into the maze of the minotaur?

Should I begin on that windy April day, on the morning when the eagles rose out of the darkness below the mighty cliffs of Ronda? When I said goodbye to my father and with my few needments under my arm climbed into the stagecoach that was to take me to Seville? But this is two years in the past and the boy I was is dim in my memory. I have even forgotten my father's shouted advice as the coach moved out of the cobbled square. That it was good advice, I am certain. Also certain is the fact that I did not heed it.

Perhaps I should begin on the day I received my diploma in cartography from the Casa de Contratación and within the hour sailed from Seville for the New World. But this too is dim in my memory, hidden beneath the fateful things that since have befallen me. As is the voyage to Vera Cruz in New Spain and the long journey to the mountain stronghold of the dead king, Montezuma.

Should I start with the day and the circumstances of my meeting with Admiral Alarcón, the oath I took to bear him fealty and of the night our fleet sailed north from Acapulco?

But what of Zia? Do not these writings truly begin with her, the Nayarit girl of the silver bells and the silvery laughter, who guided the *conducta* of Captain Mendoza into the Land of Cíbola?

5

No, I see now that the story really begins when **Admiral Alarcón** sailed into Cortés' Sea. It begins on the morning when Captain Mendoza first thought to seize command of the galleon *San Pedro*. Yes, this day is the beginning.

Through the small, barred window I can see a star. The candle sheds its good light. Now as I write of Captain Mendoza's plans to raise a mutiny and what happened to them and of the events that led me to Chichilticale, may God enlighten my mind and guide my pen!

# 1

IT WAS EIGHT BELLS of the morning watch, early in the month of June, that we entered the Sea of Cortés. On our port bow was the Island of California. To the east lay the coast of New Spain.

I sat in my cabin setting down in ink a large island sighted at dawn, which did not show on the master chart. The day was already stifling hot, so I had left the door ajar. Suddenly the door closed and I turned to face Captain Mendoza.

He glanced at the chart spread out on the table. "Is this Admiral Ulloa's?" he asked.

"A copy," I said, "which I am making as we move north."

"A true copy?"

"True, sir."

He leaned over my shoulder. "Where are we, Señor Cartographer, at the present hour?"

"This was our position yesterday at sunset." I put my finger on the chart. "We have made some twelve leagues since."

Mendoza stared down at the country that lay east and north of the spot where my finger rested. It was a vast blank space, loosely sketched. Upon it no mark showed, no river, no mountain range, no village, no city — only the single word UNKNOWN.

He turned and went to the door. I thought that he was leaving, having learned what he wished to know, but he stood there for a time and stared out at the calm sea, the white surf, the hills that rolled away to the east. Then he closed the door and leaned against it, looking down at me.

"You work hard," he said. "Your lantern burns late. I seldom encounter you."

"There is much work," I answered.

"A little sun would help. A few hours on deck. You are pale. A boy your age should move around. Not sit over a chart all day and half the night. How old are you? Seventeen? Eighteen?"

"Fifteen, sir."

"I presume from the city of Salamanca. The country of scholars, where everyone is pale, red around the eyes from reading, and has ink-stained fingers."

"No, from Ronda."

"Truly? This is difficult to believe. Those from Ronda are usually venturesome fellows. Stout with the sword. Good horsemen. Restless, ready for anything."

I looked down at the chart and the island I had not yet finished.

"Ulloa shows nothing for all of this?" he said, passing his hand across the blank space.

"Nothing," I answered. "He skirted the coast as far

8

north as the River of Good Guidance, which he discovered, but did not venture inland."

"What of Marcos de Niza and Stephen, the Moor, the ones who have seen the Seven Cities of Gold?"

"The Moor was killed at Háwikuh and his bones lie there. Father Marcos is an explorer, not a maker of maps. Neither one left a record of Cíbola nor how it was reached."

"Then the chart is of no value for those who might travel there?"

"None, sir."

"If I left the ship and set out to the east, the chart would be of no help?"

"No, sir."

"Go on with your work," Mendoza said. "The map is important. Without maps, what would we explorers do? But tell me, Señor Cartographer, about this country marked UNKNOWN. Does it not interest you to know what lies there? What glittering cities of gold and treasure?"

I nodded my head.

"But you will never see this country which is bigger than the whole of Spain or be able to draw it on a map, if you sit here in the cabin of the galleon *San Pedro*."

"I draw the coast and the islands we pass."

"The map has been drawn before. By Admiral Ulloa."

"His map I correct."

"Then you are not a maker of maps. You are one who corrects maps. A copyist."

"We sail north," I said, "perhaps into seas never charted before."

"You sail only until the moment when you sight Coronado's army. As you well know, the three galleons of this fleet are filled with supplies for that army. You also know that Coronado is marching northward along the coast, parallel to the course we follow by sea. In time, it is hoped, Admiral Alarcón shall overtake him. The ships then will pull into shore, the supplies will be unloaded and given to Coronado. You know the plan. What you do not know is this. Even if the supplies are handed over, the ships — and you with them — sail south not north. Back to Culiacán. Not into the uncharted seas you speak of."

"Alarcón may have other ideas," I said. "He may explore the Island of California and its waters."

"No, señor. He is under orders to return to Culiacán."

I could not gainsay him in this, therefore I was silent. But I began to wonder about it. I wondered about everything he had said. Why did Blas de Mendoza, a Captain in Coronado's army, who had never spoken more than a dozen words to me during the voyage, now stand in my cabin, talking as if I were a confidant?

"Here is something else you do not know, but should," he said. "Alarcón and Coronado will never meet, because the plan for their meeting is unsound. It was unsound from the start. You can see this for yourself. Many times, to avoid reefs and shallows, the ships have had to sail far from shore. True?"

"Yes, sir."

"Is it also true that because of mountains and swamps Coronado has been forced to march inland, out of sight of the sea?"

10

"Yes, sir."

"Is it possible that while one of these things took place, or both at the same time, Coronado marching inland and the ships far at sea, that the two could pass without sighting each other?"

"Yes, sir."

"It is not only possible, but it is exactly what has happened. Sometime during the last week, we have overtaken and passed Coronado. He is behind us, and yet Alarcón sails on. He sails to nowhere." Mendoza grunted in disgust. "How simple it would have been if at the start the two men had decided upon a place to meet. If Alarcón had said, 'I will sail for five days and anchor.' If Coronado had said, 'Since you sail as much in one day as my army marches in twelve, be certain that you do wait for us.'"

Mendoza was a tall man, ten years or more older than I. His eyes were dark and deep-set in a face the color of Cordovan leather, where all the bones of jaw, cheek and brow stood clear, as if after a long vigil. His clothes were elaborate. They were the furnishings of a dandy, yet beneath the lace-trimmed doublet, the fancy breeches, the shining boots was a body supple and strong as the best steel.

He gave me a searching look. "Did you sign with Alarcón to sail back and forth looking for a lost army?"

"No, sir."

"Nor did I. Yet that is our fate, unless we act."

Mendoza turned and listened at the door a moment. "Tomorrow I go ashore. I shall seize the ship and put

11

the Admiral in chains. I go in search of the Seven Golden Cities of Cíbola. In that search I have need of a good cartographer. Of someone who can take readings from the sun and stars, and thus direct our steps."

He paused and again listened at the door. "Do you join me in that search?"

I was silent.

"Or do you wish to sail back and forth in a tub?"

"I am a member of Admiral Alarcón's staff," I said.

Mendoza pretended not to hear me. He said, "Do you wish to see the Seven Cities of Cíbola? Do you wish to share in the treasure we shall find there? The gold and turquoise and silver? Surely you have heard of these fabulous riches. Or do you prefer to remain cooped in a cabin the rest of your youth while others grow rich as the richest *duque*?"

"I am a member of the crew," I said stubbornly.

"Soon there will be no crew." He opened the door and glanced fore and aft of the ship's deck. He looked back at me. "What I have said, do not repeat. But give it your thought."

With this he went on deck. Too disturbed to continue with the map I soon followed.

Under a green and gilt canopy that shielded him from the sun, Admiral Alarcón sat eating breakfast at a table spread with silver and fine linen. He was in a happy mood. He took a long drink from a flagon of Jerez. Tossing a chicken leg to the dog that lay at his feet, he raised a spyglass to look at the coast.

There was no sign he knew that a mutinous plan to

seize his ship was afoot. And yet, watching him, I wondered. Was he only biding his time?

That the ship was restless anyone could see. For more than a week it had been so. There were sailors who predicted that the *San Pedro* would sail northward to the very marge of the sea and never overtake Coronado. Some said that Admiral Alarcón had no thought of meeting him. Instead, using the supplies meant for Coronado's army, he planned to sail on to California and there search for black pearls, in which that mysterious island was rich. Bolder men said that the Admiral was a braggart, who thought more of his magnificent bronze beard than he did of his crew.

At this moment, as Admiral Alarcón sat under the green and gilt canopy enjoying his breakfast, a knot of sailors was gathered at the rail. In their midst stood Mendoza. They seemed to be scanning the coast, but from time to time I saw them glance toward the Admiral. These glances Alarcón must have noticed, but he gave no sign. He ate roundly, washing down his chicken with Jerez. At last he threw the carcass to the dog and disappeared.

I went back to my chart. But now and again I paused to watch the coastline moving past. Through the small transom I could see rust-colored hills stretching away to the east and far off against the horizon the dim shape of a mountain range. This was the country marked UN-KNOWN. Beyond it somewhere to the east lay the land called Cíbola, the country of the Seven Cities about which Captain Mendoza had spoken.

13

Cíbola I had heard of many times before. Aboard ship there was talk of little else, and in the City of Mexico, and in Seville, even in the town of Ronda men spoke of cities where the houses were fashioned of gold and the streets themselves paved with it, street after street. But these tales had meant little to me. The making of maps was the only thing I had thought of.

It was the only thing I thought of now as I sat at my table. Yet as the day wore on and the ship bore northward to the straining of blocks and the play of dolphins around us, my mind must have wandered. In less than an hour I made two unaccountable mistakes which took me long after suppertime to correct.

Night had come and the ship was quiet. The lantern swung gently in its gimbals. The map was again going well when the door opened and Captain Mendoza slipped quietly into the cabin. It was a hot night but he was muffled to the chin.

"You did not come to supper," he said, "so I bribed the cook, a greedy fellow as you know, and brought along a lamb shank."

From the folds of his cape he drew forth a well-larded bone, for which I thanked him, of a sudden very hungry.

Closing the door, he turned to look over my shoulder. "The map progresses, I see. But more than half of it, all eastward from the ocean, still remains a blank."

"It will remain so, I fear. For a time."

"You might draw in a mountain or two, at least." Mendoza said. "A few wild animals and an Indian. A river. It would make things look better all around."

"Perhaps there are no Indians there, or rivers or mountains," I said. "Possibly it is an ocean sea, like the one we sail."

Mendoza reached up and adjusted the lantern wick. I waited, thinking that he was about to speak again of the Seven Cities, new tales that I had not heard, though I had heard many.

"If I were you, if I were a cartographer," he said, "I could not rest until I beheld that vast country which you have marked with the word UNKNOWN. It would haunt me day and night, just to look at it and think that no white man had set foot there."

"It does not haunt me," I said. "But I think of it. I would like to travel and see it."

"If you do," he replied, "then no longer will it be unknown. For the map you would make of it would be published in Seville. In Paris. And Amsterdam. And London. Everywhere. Overnight you would win renown. A boy of sixteen, yet renowned in all the world."

He looked down at the map.

"What you do now has been done before," he said. "You add a little. You take away a little. Put in an island. A windrose. But still the map is much like the one made months ago during the voyage of Admiral Ulloa."

"It will be better than his," I answered, boasting.

"Yes, *señor*. But your map still remains a copy, which you must acknowledge when you come to sign your name to it."

Mendoza drew the cape around his chin. "Enjoy your

lamb shank," he said. "As you do, consider my advice."
He opened the door, scanned the deck fore and aft, then
looked at me. "And make your choice quickly, by tomorrow at the latest."

While I ate a tardy supper, the click of his heels
sounded on the deck, to and fro. When I snuffed out
the lantern and lay down in my bunk, I still could hear
them. They were the steps of one who heeded nothing,
who would grapple with anything or with anyone, be it
a ship or an officer of the King. They were the steps of
a man who would walk through the fires of hell to reach
that which he coveted.

# 2

ORNING DAWNED CLEAR with a light wind at our stern. In the night the hills had given way to a line of jagged headlands. Black tailings seemed to flow from them into the sea to rise there in reefs and rocky mounds and pinnacles. It was a desolate scene that met our eyes, and awesome to behold.

About an hour after dawn, Admiral Alarcón ordered the *San Pedro* brought up into the wind. The other two galleons of the fleet, as I remember, were astern and out of sight. He then ordered everyone to gather in the waist of the ship, those on duty and those sleeping.

With his bronze beard blowing in the wind, hands on hips, his countenance without any emotion that I could note, he faced us.

"Captain-General Coronado and his army," he said, "escape our watchful eye. Therefore, I am sending ashore a band of men to seek them out wherever they may be, east or south or north. The leader of this band is Blas de Mendoza, a captain of that lost army." He paused and made a slight bow toward Mendoza, then again addressed the crew. "All those of you who wish to join the brave captain, step forward."

I glanced at Captain Mendoza. He did not betray any emotion.

A moment before, as on the days just past, the men had been alive and restless. But now every eye among them was fixed upon the nearby coast. They stared at the angry surf, the black mounds and pinnacles, the jagged headland, and beyond at the plain that stretched endlessly away to the horizon. Down the length of the deck there was not a sound. On their faces was the look of those who for the first time gaze upon the very entrance to Inferno.

Then four stepped out, all of them soldiers who were bound to Captain Mendoza. One, Torres, was the keeper of his horses. The other three were his personal musicians, Lunes, Roa and Zuñiga. Not one of the crew followed after them.

Alarcón repeated his command, "Those who wish to join Captain Mendoza, step forward." His eyes ran through the ranks, man by man, and at last rested upon me.

For myself, I stood rooted on the deck, too surprised to move. I was not surprised that the Admiral had learned of Mendoza's plan to seize the ship. What did surprise me was that he had taken this cunning way to forestall it.

Once more, for the third time, Alarcón repeated his command. As he slowly spoke the words in a bull-like voice, his gaze ran through the ranks and again rested upon me.

Uneasily I shifted my weight. Sweat gathered on my forehead and ran down my face. I looked away from him, along the ranks of unmoving men. Gladly would I have leaped the rail into the sea.

By chance, then, my eyes met those of Captain Mendoza. He stood stiffly beside Alarcón, watching me from under his heavy lids. Of a sudden I was in the cabin and he was speaking. I heard his words clearly, as if he were speaking to me at this moment. ". . . the map you would make would be published in Seville . . . Everywhere. Overnight you would win renown. A boy of sixteen, yet renowned in all the world."

I gathered myself, and almost against my will, took one step forward.

There was a long moment of silence. Then Alarcón doffed his plumed hat, bowed low in the direction of Captain Mendoza, and strode off along the deck.

# 3

AT NOON OUR LITTLE BAND, six in all, moved away from the galleon *San Pedro*. We would have left much sooner except for the business of the horses and Captain Mendoza's clothes.

The Captain owned many changes, each of different color and cut, entire from boots to plumed hats. Each needed to be carefully packed, as well as breastplates and morions. For myself, I took only a set of instruments, cartographer's supplies, a journal, and the clothes I stood in, knowing that I must carry everything on my back.

Loading of the two horses, a blue roan from Barbary and her foal of three months, required care. Many times they were lowered over the side of the ship, up and then down, suspended from the slings in which they had traveled from Acapulco, before they were secure in the long-boat. Yet they and Torres, their keeper, were safely ashore and the boat was returning as we made ready to leave the galleon.

To mind the sails, for we were all landsmen, the Admiral sent one of his men. From the rail he called down his last instructions.

"I sail for another day and night," he shouted. "For a week I lie at anchor. Tell this to Coronado if by chance you meet."

He smiled and waved a jeweled hand. There was still no sign that he had triumphed over Mendoza. Nor did Mendoza himself show that he had been outwitted. He stood in the bow of the longboat, his jaw outthrust, and with a last prideful gesture called to his three musicians — Zuñiga who played the flute, Lunes who strummed a guitar of five strings, and Roa the drummer. At his signal the three struck up a lively tune.

The *San Pedro* dipped her flag, her crew cheered — wondrous loud, I thought, because they were not leaving — and on a light wind we moved away.

The cheers slowly faded. The galleon grew smaller on the horizon and then, as we rounded an islet, suddenly was lost to view. One by one the musicians stopped playing. Seated in the bobbing stern, my few possessions gathered around me, I stared at the place where the ship had been. I thought of my cabin and the map I had left on the table, unfinished.

Mendoza turned and swept us with a glance.

"Comrades," he said, "put the ship out of your minds. For in this life you shall never see it again. Fix your thoughts instead upon the task of getting ashore and upon the land of the Seven Golden Cities that lie beyond. And mark this well, each of you. We shall find these cities if it takes a year or five. If we walk through the soles of our boots and to live have to eat the parts that remain."

Again he signaled the musicians and turned his back upon us.

To a brisk tune we left the islet. A rocky beach lay ahead, at a distance of half a league. Beyond it a defile wound steeply upward to a treeless promontory. There against the sky I saw three small figures, Torres and the two horses.

I idly noted that the sky above them was changing from blue to white. Clouds were beginning to move through this pearly mist on a wind that did not blow here on the sea. Ulloa's sailing instructions, left behind in the cabin, I could not remember. Yet I was certain that both wind and haze were portents of foul weather, in which these seas abound.

We then came upon a series of low-lying islets. As we entered a winding corridor between them — a place of remarkable beauty where the water was clear like air and fish of every hue darted — at that very instant I heard a prolonged hiss. It was the sound of a monstrous snake.

There was a second prolonged hiss. And then in a moment's brief time came the sound of a thousand serpents venomously breathing upon us. The moving sea flattened and from its surface pellets of water, hard as stone, whipped our faces.

From my memory of Ulloa's instructions, a thought raced through my mind. June was the month of the *Chubasco,* wind with rain. Spring and Fall were the seasons of the dry *Santana.* The most dreaded wind born in all the wilderness of Cortés' Sea blew in January. This was summer but still, somehow, that wind was blowing now and we were in its path.

"*Cordonazo!*" I shouted.

The word was driven back into my throat. It made no difference. None in the longboat would have heard or understood. Wrestled to their knees by the wind, our men were trying to claw through the mound of provisions to a safer place in the bilge. Alarcón's sailor gallantly clung to the rudder.

The *Cordonazo's* first breath had parted a rope. The sail now streamed over our heads like a banner. The sailor rose to save it, but when he reached out the wind lifted him into the air. He fell upon the sea and as a man slides on the deck of a ship, so hard was the surface of the water, he slid past us and out of view.

There was no hope of saving him. Indeed, in our hearts all of us felt that we would never save ourselves. Either one by one we would be plucked from the boat by the steel fingers of the *Cordonazo,* or we would founder at once, together.

The myriad, snakelike voices of the wind became one, a scream that rose and fell and rose again. An oar, a helmet, a cask of flour, a scabbard were caught by the wind and flung into the sea.

The shore disappeared. I saw by the pale sun that we were being driven into the northwest. From what I remembered of the chart the sea was open there, free of islands and reefs upon which we could be wrecked.

We raced out of the shallows where the wind had bitten off the waves. A hill of gray water now came up behind us. Our stern lifted high and we sank downward, downward until it seemed that we must founder on the bare rocks beneath the sea.

At this moment Captain Mendoza crawled the length of the boat and wrapped his arms around the tiller. But for this we would have drowned. As it was, the longboat listed and began to fill with water.

We bailed, using our helmets, until our hands bled. We bailed through the afternoon, never stopping. The sun went down and still we bailed, except Roa the drummer who lay as if dead.

A star showed in the east. It was small and wan, yet it proved an omen of good fortune. The wind lessened and began to blow in gusts. The moon rose in a sky swept clean of mist, turning the gray waves to silver.

For a time it was quiet, yet we waited. We looked at the sky, the sea, at each other, not believing that the *Cordonazo* had blown itself out and that we were still alive.

With the toe of his boot Captain Mendoza aroused Roa. "Drummer," he said, "a tune. Something of a lively nature."

Roa stirred himself and rose from the bilge. "The drum has grown soggy," he said.

"Play," the captain said.

While three of us bailed and Mendoza held the rudder, Roa beat his drum. The sound was hollow, but as we drifted into the north it served to enliven us.

# 4

$\mathcal{T}$HE WAVES GREW SMALLER in the night. Taking turns, two men bailing while the others slept, we kept the longboat dry. At dawn the sea was calm. By the early light we surveyed the storm's damage.

My first thought was for the maps and instruments, which I had carefully wrapped when we left the *San Pedro* and placed between two bags of flour. The flour was wet, but to my great relief the roll was safe, uninjured by the sea water.

Our swords and daggers, we found, were already beginning to rust. One of Mendoza's cloaks was gone, besides a small sack of trinkets we had brought for barter with the Indians. The oar and sail, however, blown away in the first blast of the wind, were our most grievous loss.

"We have been driven afar," Mendoza said, looking at the instruments I held in my lap. "How far, Maker of Maps?"

"It is impossible to tell until noon," I said. "Then I shall take a reading on the sun."

"What is your guess?"

"Ten leagues."

"How far away is the coast?"

"Perhaps five leagues."

"Then we should see it."

"Not from our height, unless there were mountains on the coast," I said, explaining to him that since the world was proven round the horizon lowered five *varas* every half league.

He did not wait to hear me out. "We head for the coast," he said, and gave orders for the stitching of a sail.

The sail was a makeshift, two blankets sewed together, yet it served to catch what wind there was. With it and the aid of our one oar, we set a course to eastward.

At noon we took our first water that day, drinking little from the goatskin Mendoza passed around. Our throats soon were parched again, for the sun shone fiercely upon us. It fell upon us like fiery rain. It struck the sea and shattered into a thousand barbs of light that blinded our eyes and seared our flesh.

At dusk we sighted land low on the horizon.

About the same time, sitting at the oar, I noted that the boat left no wake and that we were moving north-by-east in a crablike motion. It was as if the whole sea were flowing away from the land.

"I remember that Ulloa's chart speaks of strong currents in this part of the sea," I told Mendoza, "caused by the difference between high and low tide, often as much as twenty feet. We must be caught in such a current. Furthermore, the chart warns that a boat cannot move against these tides, but must go with them until they run their course."

Mendoza glanced at the coast, less than a league away. His face hardened and I could see that he meant to reach it. Jumping to his feet, he reset the sail to catch more wind and shouted for Zuñiga to help me at the oar.

"Pull, you sons of Spain!" he shouted.

And pull we did until our eyes started from their sockets. The heavy longboat did not change direction. Mendoza pushed me aside and took my place at the oar. Yet the boat sped onward with the powerful tide, farther and farther from the coast.

Until midnight the tide held fast. Then, as you open your hand and free a bird, it released us.

At this time, using the Pole Star, I found its elevation above the sea and thus our position, south and north. (Someday a man wise in these matters will think of a trustworthy way to tell distance east and west. Even now, I have heard, there is a navigator in Portugal who claims to have invented such a method. Would that he had been with us on the Sea of Cortés!)

"We have been carried back," I told Mendoza, "almost to the place I fixed at noon."

"But how far is the coast?" he demanded.

"That I do not know."

"A cartographer and you cannot tell right from left?"

I tried to explain to him why this was difficult, but turning his back, he raised the sail and again we set toward the east.

We were too tired to row, so we ate a few biscuits, took sips of water, and lay down to sleep, all of us except Captain Mendoza. He sat at the tiller, holding the goatskin of water, which was now half-empty, between his knees.

The sun seemed to grow hotter. We dug small caves among the baggage to lie in when we were not rowing. We drank no water until midday and then only one mouthful apiece.

Low yellow cliffs marched along beside us and a heavy surf beat against them. Through the afternoon we watched for a soft place to land, but saw none.

Night came and we sailed slowly on into the north. In the morning the yellow cliffs were still there. Fog hung over the sea but the sun quickly bore through it and sought us out.

We now were too exhausted to row, so we lay in our caves and came out only to take turns at the tiller.

We passed close to a small island covered with birds. They stood motionless as the longboat sailed by, their red beaks hanging open in the heat.

From the south white clouds rolled up and the wind died to a whisper.

"Tell us, scanner of the heavens, reader of charts," Mendoza said. "Tell us what Ulloa has about clouds."

The words were thick for his mouth was swollen from the sun, like all our mouths.

"He says that it rains during the summer in the Sea of Cortés," I answered. "Sometimes for a week."

"We have been five days on the sea and it has not rained."

"I have counted," Lunes said, "it is six days, not five."

Mendoza shrugged his shoulders.

I was surprised at Lunes because he was not one to

argue. I was more surprised at the Captain's silence, for no one argued with him, even over a trifle.

The clouds rose higher. From time to time I saw Lunes glance at the goatskin of water, which the Captain held between his knees. Suddenly he staggered up and pointed into the west.

"Three galleons," he cried.

Everyone got to his feet.

"I see nothing," said Zuñiga, who had a squint and saw little at any time.

"All with sails flying," Lunes said. "Look, where I point."

I shaded my eyes and looked until tears ran down my cheeks and dried there. I saw nothing except the steaming sea.

"You have lost your wits," Roa said and sat down.

"Next you will see lakes and trees growing beside them," Zuñiga said.

Mendoza laughed, though there was little to laugh at. "A mirage," he said. "A moment ago I saw waterfalls. I conjured them because I wished to."

"Lunes, you see so much, can you see Admiral Alarcón eating a breakfast of cold fowl?" Roa asked. "Does he drink Jerez or Madeira?"

Lunes fell silent. He sat down and again began to eye the goatskin.

The white clouds moved overhead and formed themselves into snow-covered mountains. Rearing above the mountains were great castles and battlements and below them were running horses and fighting men. After a time, when the sun set, it gilded the roofs of the castles with gold and the gold sifted down over everything.

"The Seven Cities," Lunes said, watching the clouds. "All gold. Even the doors and the tiles people walk upon."

"Captain," Roa said, "is there much water in the Seven Golden Cities?"

"Springs and rivulets, streams and rivers and lakes of water," Mendoza answered. "And fountains everywhere, tall as the trees along the Guadalquivir in our city of Seville."

"Tell us more about the fountains," Zuñiga said.

"I cannot talk more of fountains or of anything," Mendoza answered. "My lips are very sore. Words feel like burning pebbles in my throat."

"This is the way with all of us," said Roa. "But I too wish to hear more of the fountains."

Mendoza was silent.

Lunes said, "There is also true gold in the streets which lead to the castles. Paved with golden flagstones so heavy that it needs two men to lift just one."

Mendoza picked up the goatskin but did not pass it around. He held it and gave each of us a sip of water and put the stopper back.

"Musicians," he said, "we now play a tune. Something gay to suit the circumstance."

Roa found his drum and Zuñiga his fife. The sun had given Lunes' guitar the shape of a gourd, but together the three played a tune that was gay and also sad. It was the same tune Don Baltasar, my grandfather, had marched to when he fought the Moors at the siege of Granada.

# 5

ARKNESS CAME and we moved northward. I remember nothing of this night. Nor much of the day which followed, except that I thought death was not far away. It was just beyond the horizon. It was there waiting for me because I had broken my solemn pledge to Admiral Alarcón.

The sun rose in a cloudless sky, the same as before. We passed a large island without grass or tree or bush. The sun was a leech that sucked the moisture from our flesh.

That night I remember well.

At dusk the Captain gave us a sip of water and each a biscuit. Little water was left in the goatskin, but this he guarded, putting the goatskin between his knees, his sword within reach.

It was quiet and the moon had risen when I heard behind me on the sea a thin, dry sound, like a knife cutting through silk. The sound grew louder and drew abreast of the boat and I saw a dark fin glide past. It curved away into the night, leaving a trail of phosphorescence. Another fin cut through the water and a third.

Shortly thereafter, Lunes crawled to where I lay in the bow. He put his mouth close to my ear. "The Captain sleeps," he whispered. "I will take his sword and the goatskin. Then we row to the shore. It is near. Listen. Hear the surf?"

"The boat would founder," I said. "We would lose everything."

"You wish to die here?"

"Better this than the other."

Lunes leaned across the rail and put his hand in the water. He rose to his knees and said something I could not hear. Again he leaned over the rail and before I could stop him he had slipped into the sea and was swimming slowly away from the boat.

I called to Mendoza, but he was already awake.

"Let him go," he said. "His kind we do not need."

I watched Lunes swim down the moon's path, a spot that grew small and was lost at last from view. Once more I heard the sound of knives cutting through silk.

I lay down and closed my eyes but did not sleep. Time passed, perhaps an hour. There was movement in the stern of the longboat. It was Mendoza. He held the goatskin above his head and was drinking.

He put down the goatskin. "Do you sleep, conceiver of maps?" he said.

I did not answer, not wanting him to know that I had seen.

"You are awake," he said. "I have heard before the sounds you make while sleeping. You wonder why I drink the water and fail to share it with you."

I remained silent. I could not have spoken had I wished to.

"You do not ask the question of me," he said. "But I will tell you. By drinking I save my own life and thus shall you save yours. For without me, you perish. Furthermore, I have consumed all the water, only a mouthful, but the last. This is for you to know. Not Zuñiga. Not Roa. This is a secret between us."

It is true, I thought as I lay there in the bow of the longboat. Only he has kept us alive, through the storm and the terrible days since. Without him the boat would have foundered, or we would have gone mad, like Lunes, or fought among ourselves, but somehow perished.

As I listened to him in silence, the suspicion crossed my mind that he was thinking only of himself, of saving his own life, not ours. It was a treacherous act, which I, who had broken my pledge to Admiral Alarcón would not have done. Or so I told myself, not knowing that the dream of gold can bend the soul and even destroy it, unaware that one day it would do the same to me.

Mendoza fell silent. The boat drifted northward on a slow tide. Everything about us was silver, moon-bright and shimmering.

During the night the sea changed. It was now the color of parchment, with dark streaks running through and fronds of a weedlike plant floating. The cliffs had gone and there were low dunes instead, rolling away to the east. Mendoza reset the ragged sail and changed course toward them. There was no wind, so he picked up the oar and began to row, the rest of us too weak to help.

We moved slowly across the flat water, which soon glittered like a burnished shield. None of us thought that he would ever reach the land. One by one, except for Captain Mendoza, we prayed aloud to San Nicolás of Mira and committed ourselves to God.

Clouds came up in the south. Again they reared themselves and formed castles and battlements, but no one spoke of them.

Of a sudden Roa staggered to his feet. He was very fat and it took him a while to do so. "I die of thirst," he cried. "There is fire in my throat."

Crouching, he moved toward Mendoza, who held the empty goatskin in his lap.

"We drink at noon," Mendoza said. He stopped rowing and grasped his sword. "At noon, only."

Roa glanced at the sword. He took a step backward, muttering, then threw himself across the rail and began to claw the water. I tried to pull him back but he wrestled free. With a lunge he was out of the boat, to flounder in the sea, drinking mouthfuls of sea water from cupped hands.

He stopped drinking. He looked up at me and a strange light came into his eyes.

"Water," he cried. "Fresh water!"

It was a hoarse, unearthly cry that rang in my ears, the cry of a man demented.

Mendoza held out the oar and shouted for him to take it. Roa did not heed the command. He rolled over on his back and let the sea water pour into his mouth. He made wild, choking sounds, flailing his arms. Then he grew quiet and paddled to the boat and asked for his helmet.

I found the helmet and leaned over the rail, ready to grasp him. As I handed it down, Roa eluded me. Shouting a jumble of words, he dipped the helmet half-full and held it up. Mendoza took the helmet, while I managed to seize Roa's outstretched arm.

"Drink!" Roa cried.

Mendoza put the rim of the morion to his lips, for no other reason, I am sure, than to humor him. The next instant the Captain threw back his head and let the water pour over his face. He laughed and took a drink and laughed again. He handed me the morion. With one leap he was in the sea, rolling over and over like a dolphin.

The water was cool to my lips, as fresh as if it had come from a deep well in the earth. I gulped it again. Suddenly I remembered a note from Ulloa's chart, which said that at the mouth of the River of Good Guidance, where the river emptied into Cortés' Sea, in that place there existed a small lake of fresh water.

Since dawn when I first saw that the sea had changed color, we had been drifting on this lake. And by some great good fortune, by a miracle, during the time when the tide was at ebb. For at high tide, so Ulloa had noted, the sea raced into the river mouth and the lake of sweet water disappeared.

Yes, through a miracle, we were floating at the mouth of the very river, upon the very lake of sweet water, which Admiral Ulloa had discovered.

*The Fortress of San Juan de Ulúa*
*Vera Cruz, in New Spain*
*The twenty-fourth day of September*
*The year of our Lord's birth, 1541*

THE JAILER HAS FINISHED his nightly rounds and I can hear the clanking of keys as he climbs the stairs. He has brought my supper, but of more importance, a new sheaf of paper. While my memory is still fresh I can write down everything that has happened to me this day, my seventh day in prison, the day before my trial begins.

About mid-morning Don Felipe comes to my cell. "The Royal Audiencia has appointed counsel to defend you," he says. "The gentleman is waiting above." He hands me a comb and a sharp razor. "You cannot go to meet him looking like a picker of rags."

As I start to shave myself, Don Felipe says, "When you talk with the counsel, guard what you say. His concern for your guilt or innocence is small. His real concern lies elsewhere. In the treasure. About that, everything he can pry from you he will pry. So speak little, *señor,* and this with caution. Likewise, remember that a trial before the Audiencia is not like other trials you may know about. The Audiencia makes its own rules. If you remember this, it will save you confusion."

We climb the stairs together, Don Felipe's two Indians at our heels. After twelve steps we come to a broad landing and a sentry box. In the doorway a man with a pointed beard leans on a musket. As I follow Don Felipe across the landing, I hear the sound of voices beneath me. They come from a row of narrow, iron-barred openings cut into the stone.

"Prisoners," Don Felipe says. "Their food is let down by rope. We have other cells, even smaller, so small that a man can crouch but cannot stand. Others that are mere holes in the sea-wall, half-flooded at high tide. And the large hole. In this one a dozen men stand with their arms through rings in the wall, while the tide creeps up to their chins, twice each day."

In his voice there is a tone of pride, an ominous tone as well. "In all of them," he says, "men die in a few weeks or go insane. So you see, *caballero,* how truly fortunate you are."

At the end of the landing is a second flight of twelve stairs and this leads to a broad esplanade. Beyond a stretch of water are the red roofs of the City of the True Cross. Everything I behold is new to me, for I was brought to the fortress at night.

We cross the esplanade to a stone tower and Don Felipe leads the way into a small, dingy room where a young man is seated. He is scarcely older than I am, perhaps twenty or twenty-one. His name is Pablo Gamboa and he wears a clean but threadbare doublet, trimmed with ragged lace at cuffs and throat. Both his age and his poverty discomfort me.

In a thin, undernourished voice, after a polite greeting, he says, "To the charge of defrauding his Majesty, the King, do you wish to plead guilty or not guilty?"

"Guilty," I answer.

This takes him aback. His eyes, which are large and hungry, grow larger. "Then you did defraud the King of his rightful share of treasure, which you have in your possession, and so wish to plead?"

"The treasure is not in my possession."

"Where is it?" the counsel asks.

"In the land of the Seven Cities," I reply, remembering Don Felipe's admonition.

"If this is the case," he says, "the matter is simple. Give the King his royal share of this treasure and I shall ask clemency for you."

"The treasure is hidden," I answer. "Forever."

"What do you mean?"

"I mean that it is hidden in a secret place and hidden there where no man will ever find it."

"Then you do not wish to give the King his share?"

"No."

Counsel Gamboa looks at his fingers, which are thin and sallow, and after a moment at me. He seems to think I am mad.

"Peculiar," he mumbles. "How do I present your case to the Royal Audiencia? And ask clemency for one who deliberately defies the King?"

"I do not defy the King. I refuse to tell where the gold is hidden. That is all."

"For what reason?"

"For a reason that is my own. Which can be of no interest to the King or to the Royal Audiencia."

Counsel Gamboa shakes his head. Now it is clear he thinks that he is dealing with a madman. He asks me if I am aware of the severe penalties for the crime I have committed. When I answer that I am, he again shakes his head and escorts me to the door, saying that he will give my case his closest attention.

While we walk back to my cell, Don Felipe, who has listened outside the door, commends me for not betraying the gold's whereabouts. But we are no sooner in the cell with the iron door closed than he turns a different face.

"The map," he says, "How does it proceed?"

"Slowly. In my mind, only."

"In your mind?" He takes two steps toward me. "You were in the land of Cíbola. There you found a great treasure and there you hid it. Since you are a cartographer you would have made careful notes. The degrees of latitude, certain features of the landscape — rocks, streams, hills, mountains — concerning this hiding place. These notes you must have."

"I have notes on the country. But not of the hiding place. They are in Mexico City."

"Where?" Don Felipe picks up the candle and holds it close to my face, as if it will help him to tell whether or not I speak the truth. "Where in the City of Mexico?"

"Near the Zócolo," I answer. "A *fonda* called The Three Brothers. I left them there with the proprietor the day I was brought to Vera Cruz."

Don Felipe puts down the candle.

"I send a messenger to this inn," he says. "Within six days or less he will return. If he returns without the notes, then, *señor*, you shall spend the rest of your days in a hole. First in one where we let down food on a rope. Then, if you are still alive, in the deep one where the tide flows in and out."

"The notes might have been stolen," I protest. "Or lost. The Three Brothers is not the safest place in the City of Mexico."

"Stolen? Lost? Could a thief tell from the notes where the gold is hidden? Could anyone tell?"

"No. They can be read by me only."

"Excellent! Now pray. Pray that the notes remain safe."

He walks to the door and opens it, but then changes his mind and closes it again. He goes to a corner of the cell and there on his knees claws loose a stone. Below it is a second stone, a third, beneath the three an opening large enough to conceal a small bundle.

"Use this," he says, putting back the stones, "to hide the map you will make. And also the journal you keep."

I do not tell him that already I have found an opening in the wall, better than the one in the floor, where I now hide the journal.

The same star shines beyond the window. Its name I should know, but do not. The sea is calm. Far below me I hear the moans of some poor wretch. Now, before my trial begins tomorrow, I can write of our meeting with Zia and Father Francisco, of the forgotten city of Chichilticale, and the old man's prophetic curse.

# 6

HERE AT THE MOUTH of the mighty River of Good Guidance, where its waters pour into the Sea of Cortés, we drank our fill and more. Still too weak to climb into the longboat, clinging to rail and rudder, we then paddled feebly toward a row of sand dunes.

After a while, when it seemed that we would never reach the shore, friendly currents gathered us in. They bore us into a salt lagoon where long-legged birds were wading and, gently as a mother with her child, set us down.

We rested two days beside the lagoon, gaining strength. Early on the third morning we shouldered our baggage and set out to the southeast. We went in this direction for two reasons. Directly to the east, which was the way to Cíbola or so Captain Mendoza thought, the country was broken by sea-swamps and estuaries. Of more importance was the fact that somehow we must find Juan Torres and the horses. Knowing that we had been driven northward by the storm, he would probably follow the coast in the hope of crossing our trail.

On the morning of the fifth day, having made only nine leagues with our heavy burdens, it was decided to send Roa ahead on the chance that he would come upon a village where he could ask for help.

It is said by the poor of Seville that good fortune is like bread — sometimes a whole loaf and sometimes none.

This was our time of good fortune. No sooner had we encamped that afternoon than we saw smoke rising from a canyon nearby. In a short time Roa with three Indians came out to greet us and lead the way into a village of many huts, which was called Avipa.

Good fortune was still with us.

At the far end of the village a crowd stood in a wide circle around a mounted Spaniard. It was Juan Torres, blacksmith, armorer and keeper of Mendoza's two horses. As he saw us and spurred the roan to a gallop, the crowd of Indians scattered in all directions, letting out unearthly cries of fear.

"I never thought to see you again," he said, swinging down from the saddle. "Yet I am in the village no more than a moment when who comes running out of a hut but Benito Roa."

"You should not be so happy to see us," Zuñiga said. "For now we place our baggage on the roan. While you, *señor*, walk like the rest of us."

"To walk is good," Torres said, "after the leagues I have ridden. It was like riding the length of Spain, *amigos*."

Torres was a small man, with a glib tongue and eyes that did not rest for long on anything. I had seldom seen him on board the *San Pedro,* but what I had seen I had not fancied.

"Many adventures have befallen me," he said, "of which I will tell you once I have eaten."

"We are not without adventures ourselves," said Mendoza.

We made camp on a stream outside the village and were brought a fine supper of rabbit roasted on a spit, small squash and lemon-colored melons which surprised the tongue with their sweetness. While we ate, a group of Indians sat outside the circle of our fire, saying nothing. Now and again one would get up and walk over to where the horses were tethered, grunt something to himself, then come back and sit in silence.

"We will mount guard tonight," Mendoza said. "And those not guarding will sleep with their eyes open."

The first watch was mine. The moon had risen and I was walking along the stream, matchlock on my shoulder, when a shout and the barking of dogs brought me to a halt. There was another shout, the flare of a second torch, the sound of what seemed like iron-shod hooves striking stone. I went to awaken the camp, but Mendoza, Zuñiga and Roa already were running toward the village.

Unsure of what I had heard, fearing an attack, I doubled back to guard the roan and her foal. I was there only a short time before three horsemen rode out of the village and down the stream, light from torches shining on their helmets. They were followed by an Indian youth and a priest in a robe tucked up to his knees.

The party, we learned, belonged to Coronado's army.

They had been sent to search for Admiral Alarcón and had traveled for three days from a valley where Coronado was now encamped. The leader of the party, Ensign Gómez, told us that for a month before reaching the valley the army had marched on half rations.

"The sheep began to lose their hooves and were left behind. The pigs became little save bristle and bone. Cows and mules died. Men died, too. At last, in desperation, Coronado decided to leave the main army to travel at its own pace and push ahead with an advance guard of a hundred. He is now encamped in a valley where food and water and grass are plentiful and the Indians friendly. Still, a long journey lies between us and Cíbola. We can use the supplies Alarcón carries."

"Where the Admiral is, I do not know," Mendoza said and described the fearful storm. "If his galleons were not sunk, they were driven ashore some place."

As he said this, Mendoza glanced at me. It was a warning to be silent. It commanded me not to tell what I knew — that Admiral Alarcón planned to sail for two days after we left him, then anchor and wait for Coronado.

"Could he have found his way into the River of Good Guidance?" Gómez asked.

"We were at the mouth of that river. We have just come from there and did not sight him," Mendoza replied. "It is my belief that his ships foundered in the same storm that overtook us."

"But it is possible that they rode out the storm," Gómez said. "As you did."

"If so, where are they? How do we find them on such

a vast sea? And if by chance we do find them, what is the condition of the food they carry?"

Once more, Captain Mendoza glanced at me, commanding my silence.

He is the leader of our party, I told myself, my superior. I cannot contradict what he has said. And if I do inform Gómez about Alarcón's plans, it will be of no value because the storm has surely changed them. Besides, everything the Captain has said is true. The ships are probably lost. If not lost, then the supplies they carry are damaged beyond use. Furthermore, if the ships are still afloat, where are they?

This was what I told myself, as I stood listening to the two men. But now, while I sit at my bench and write what I remember of that night in Avipa, I know that all of it was meant to excuse my silence. I was anxious, nay, in a state of great excitement, to reach the country of Cíbola, like Mendoza but for a different reason. The only thought I had was of the map I would draw of its Seven Golden Cities, the map that no one ever had drawn before.

"If the ships are not at the bottom of the sea," I said, "which seems likely, how many weeks will it take to find them?"

It was an idle question, meant for Gómez, but Mendoza was quick to answer.

"I will tell you," he said. "By the time they are found, if find them we do, and pack animals are collected and the supplies loaded and carried back to camp, by that time snow will have fallen."

"Coronado has been on the trail many months," I said. "He must long to set foot in Cíbola."

"When the cordillera is covered with snow," Mendoza continued, "the army cannot move forward until spring."

I walked away and left the two men arguing. They argued far into the night, but at dawn we set off for Coronado's camp. There was no power on earth that could have held Mendoza back, nor, alas, held me.

# 7

THE VILLAGE WAS AWAKE as we moved away, more to see the horses than us Spaniards. Indians stood in the doorways of their huts, peering out in fear and wonder at the long-legged beasts. Beside one of the huts I saw a flock of turkeys, and thinking of the paints I would need to mix for my maps, I stopped to ask if I could buy four or five eggs.

The old woman who owned the flock understood my motions of a turkey in the act of laying. I felt very foolish stooping in the dust, but when I held up five fingers and showed her a trinket, she fetched me a fine clutch of eggs, brown-speckled and still warm. I would have preferred the newly-laid eggs of a hen, but there were none of these birds in the village.

Ensign Gómez and two soldiers rode in the lead. Mendoza rode behind them on the blue roan, the foal at her heels. The slender Indian youth and the priest, Father Francisco, who had a crooked leg and walked lopsided, followed. Zuñiga, Roa and I came last. Our baggage had been loaded upon the pack animals, so for a time we kept up with the train.

At a safe distance a band of curious Indians ran along beside us. But at the brow of the first hill they disappeared into the brush. The youth made a gesture toward them, which I took to be impolite, then left the trail and waited for me, laughing.

"Why do you laugh?" I asked.

"Because of the Indians," the youth answered. "Those who have hidden in the brush. Those who have not seen a horse before."

"You are very young," I said. "You cannot have seen many yourself."

"I have thirteen years and two hundred and six days and I have seen horses before. Dozens of horses. Horses of all the colors." He cast a glance toward Mendoza. "But I have seen no horse so beautiful as the one the captain rides. It is the color of a rain cloud, just before the rain falls. And the little one is beautiful also. I would like to ride on its back someday."

"It is not ready to ride," I said.

"Someday."

"When it is, you cannot ride it," I said. "Do you know why?"

"I know why. It is because of a man whose name was Cortés. He was the man who killed all the Aztecs. When he had killed them he made a law that no Indian can own a horse. Or ride upon a horse. This is true?"

"It is true."

The youth looked sidewise at me and laughed again.

"Do you know what the Indians of Avipa asked me, just before they ran and hid in the brush?"

I shook my head.

"They said that these animals have very big teeth, so with such teeth they must eat people. I said yes, they ate people, but they liked to eat Indians best."

"That is why they ran off?"

"Yes, but this is good. These ones of Avipa are fine at stealing. While you talk they steal from you. They pick up things with their toes, which are like fingers, and hide them away in their clouts. In front of your eyes, they do this."

The youth spoke Spanish clearly, though with long pauses and curious sounds between each word.

"Where did you learn my language?" I said.

"I learned from Captain Coronado. Also, before that, in the house of Don Alesandro, who is the Alcalde of Compostela, where I was a maid for his children, of which he has nine."

"A maid?" I said, surprised. "How can a boy be a maid?"

"I am not a boy. My name is Zia."

Zia was thin, all arms and legs, straight as a stick, tall for thirteen years, two hundred and six days, with birdlike bones and eyes that were sometimes melting. Now as she looked at me they were the color of obsidian.

"In all your life have you heard of a boy named Zia?" she said.

49

"No, nor of a girl called by that name."

"Then you have not heard of much," she said.

The next moment she was gone, skipping ahead over the rocks. But before long she came running back.

"Where," she said, "have you learned the language you speak? It does not sound the same as the language of Captain Coronado. Or the language of Don Alesandro."

"In the country of Spain. In a town named Ronda, where I was born."

"In that country does everyone speak this language?"

"Yes, but there are many dialects. Many ways of speaking, as you have just said."

"Here, also, there are many ways."

"How many do you know?"

"Six," Zia said proudly and named them one by one on her fingers. "But I do not know much of what they speak in Avipa. It sounds like the fighting of cats."

Zia wore a deerskin jacket and around her waist, cinched with a belt of woven string, a red velvet kirtle that looked as if it had been fashioned from a soldier's cast-off cloak. But it was her hat that caught my eye. From the rim hung balls of red wool, intermingled with small silver bells that tinkled as she walked.

"Is this the hat of your country?" I said.

"Yes, of Nayarit, which is close to the town of Compostela. Do you wish to hear me speak of it?"

Before I could answer and for the next league or more, she told me about Nayarit, of her father who had died soon after she was born, of her mother, who was a seamstress for Coronado and had sickened and died and was buried on the trail near Culiacán.

"Have you come like the others to find gold in the Land of Cíbola?" she asked. "Do you talk about gold and dream of it?"

"No."

"Why not? The others do."

"Because I am a cartographer, a maker of maps. And therefore I dream of maps. Do you understand what I mean by map?"

"I have seen one, which belongs to Captain Coronado." She glanced at the roll under my arm. "These are maps that you carry?"

"Maps and the colors to make them," I said. "Paper and ink, brushes and pens."

"Sometime I would like to see these maps."

"Sometime I will show them to you."

"Now?"

"Later."

"When we come to Coronado's camp?"

"Then."

She looked at me to make certain that I meant what I had said. Then from a pocket in her skirt she took a small, ratlike creature, with long back legs, and held it up in the palm of her hand.

"What is it?" I asked.

"An aguatil. It lives in the deserts and never needs to drink water. It does not like water. It's name is Montezuma."

I doubted her story but it was true. In the days to

come, when horses and men thirsted, this ratlike creature thrived, getting by some means from the seeds it ate, the water it needed.

"Now that I have shown you my pet," she said, "I wish to see the maps."

"Later."

"At Coronado's camp?"

"Yes."

Thrusting Montezuma back into her pocket, she ran with skips and jumps toward the head of the column.

Our way led through fields of cactus and we went slowly. Many of these plants were like trees, in the shape of a cross, tall as a man on horseback. Others looked like small barrels, others like friendly bushes. But all were covered with secret spines or claws, needle-sharp and painful to the touch.

Mendoza rode back to urge us on. At his heels trotted a big greyhound with yellow eyes and lean, powerful jaws. Gómez had brought the dog with him and I had seen it skulking around our camp in Avipa.

"How do you like Tigre?" he asked me. "I have just bought him from Gómez. I only paid one peso, a bargain, huh?"

"His tail is worth that," I said. It was, indeed, for it was very long and lashed the air in great sweeps. "A good bargain."

"He has one fault, however," Mendoza admitted. "He was trained to attack Indians. Instead, as things have turned out, he likes them better than Spaniards. But I will give him a few lessons and change his ideas."

From time to time during the morning, Mendoza returned to spur us on, yet by noon we had made only three short leagues. It was then that he decided to ride ahead with Gómez and the soldiers, leaving the rest of us to follow at our own pace.

"Now we travel as we wish," Father Francisco said when the others left us. "Now we get to see the country we pass through. What lives here, what crawls and walks and flies, what grows around us. We can look at the hills and mountains and watch the clouds with quiet eyes."

The cactus fields disappeared, but because of Father Francisco our progress was slow. He was forever darting off the trail at his lopsided trot to gather some leaf or flower or insect, which he carefully stowed in a leather bag. Spare as the wooden cross he carried slung over his back, four times my age, yet he was stronger than I and tireless.

Despite Father Francisco, we came at nightfall of the third day to the brow of a high, tree-covered hill. Through the trees, far below I saw a nest of flickering lights no larger than my hand.

"Coronado's army," Zia said. "Before half the night is gone, we will be there among the fires."

But the rest of us were too tired to go farther, except Father Francisco, so we camped on the hill, and feasted on dried deer meat and melons. Afterwards we sat looking down at Coronado's camp and the dim land rolling away to the north.

I asked Zia what she knew of the country beyond, the land beyond the mountains I had seen at nightfall.

"I have been to this valley twice before," she said. "I came with my uncle and we brought parrots of every color to trade for silver, which is found in this valley. I have not been farther, but I know tales of the land beyond. The place of Cíbola and the Seven Golden Cities."

"Tell me what you have heard," I said. "Not of the gold for already I have heard much."

Roa said, "No, tell us of the gold."

"Of the gold," Zuñiga said.

Zia turned to me. "Do you wish to know about the country beyond the mountains so you can make a picture?"

"No."

"I will bring the roll, which has the paper and brushes and paint and other things."

"Until I have seen the country with my own eyes, I cannot make a picture."

"Then why do you wish me to speak about it?" Zia said.

"Because," Father Francisco broke in, "he has curiosity, though not so much as you have. You have enough for ten girls."

I learned little from Zia that night, for in the middle of a sentence she yawned and fell asleep.

Not long after, I dreamed that I was among mountains of surpassing beauty, where pines grew tall and high waterfalls tumbled through crystal air. And when I went to find my paints and brushes they were gone. Zia had stolen them and was running away so fast through the trees that I could not catch her.

# 8

WITH THE FIRST LIGHT we descended. The valley was still in darkness but here and there breakfast fires were burning. As we dropped lower, I could see men busy in the camp, strings of horses and mules and burros on their way to water, children and their mothers washing at a spring.

When the sun was an hour high we were still threading our way downward through heavy brush. Voices and the neighing of horses drifted up to us. A trumpet blared, an echo answered from the hills. Suddenly, like a great serpent uncoiling, the mass took shape, the bright coils lengthened, and the shape became a moving army.

In the lead rode a man in gilded cuirass and helmet with a tall, black plume.

"The one who rides first," Zia said, "is Captain Coronado. From here you cannot see, but he has a red beard with curls in it."

Behind Coronado rode his officers and the servants, pages, and extra mounts. Five priests came next, carrying crosses. Next came a column of foot soldiers, many bands of Indians and their wives and children, pigs, flocks of sheep, and a line of pack animals.

As the leaders passed below us, Roa pointed to a horseman in a yellow doublet. He cupped his hands and shouted, *"Hola."*

It was Captain Mendoza. Mounted on the roan, he sat erect, holding aloft a banner which he had brought from Spain, which I had carried on my back from the River of Good Guidance to the village of Avipa — a yellow unicorn on a field of green.

*"Hola,"* we shouted together.

Mendoza glanced up and at last saw us where we stood shoulder-deep in the brush. He pulled his horse aside and with a sweep of his hand waved us down.

We scrambled and slid but did not reach the bottom of the hill until the army had passed. Mendoza was spurring his horse around in circles. He was as restless as he had been on the ship.

"You travel like old women," he called. "At this pace we shall never leave the valley. Tomorrow I will buy horses and three of you can ride. He looked down at his musicians and shouted, "Play!"

Dutifully Roa beat his drum, Zuñiga blew his flute, Zia, Father Francisco and I fell in behind them, and with Captain Mendoza leading us, we marched forward like a regular little army. We overtook a few stragglers and a woman riding a mule, a boy seated behind her.

"That one," Zia whispered to me, "is Señora Hozes. Her husband is a page of Coronado. She thinks the army belongs to her. When she speaks, and she speaks much, her husband listens like a dumb man. Captain Coronado listens also, but he smiles when he does."

The woman had a lean face and a cold eye. She looked at me and said, "More mouths to feed." She looked at Roa and Zuñiga, listened a moment to their playing, then put a finger in each ear.

We hurried forward, until we reached a place near the head of the column. There we fell in behind our captain. The day was cloudless. The valley sloped gently upward toward dim mountains. The sun shone bright on helmet and breastplate. Banners fluttered in the wind. I could scarce wait until the time when I might draw all that I saw on paper.

Late that afternoon we camped on the banks of a stream where water ran warm and maize flourished. Indians who called themselves Pimas came before long, carrying large trays woven of grass.

On the trays, laid out in rows festooned with fern leaves, were the hearts of deer and rabbits, doves and owls, even the small hearts of hummingbirds. These trays they offered to Coronado and his officers, bidding them to eat.

When Coronado held back, a guide explained the meaning of the gifts, which was to give strength and courage for his long journey.

Coronado took one of the hearts from a tray, a small one, but did not eat it. With a flourish he doffed his plumed hat and raised his sword.

"In the name of Charles the Fifth," he said, "I accept this wondrous gift. Henceforth, as a token of my thankfulness, your fair home shall be known to all Spaniards as the Valley of Hearts."

The friendly Pimas urged Coronado to rest by their stream. High mountains and deep canyons lay beyond, they said, and many hardships. But he was impatient to move on, so at dawn we broke camp, following the stream in a northerly direction.

True to his word, Mendoza had purchased three horses from one of the officers. On this morning, to our great delight, Roa, Zuñiga, and I rode. Zia could not ride because of Cortés' law, and Father Francisco, in true apostolic fashion, desired to walk.

Mendoza was again restless as we started off, thinking that the army should take a shorter route. "We are marching back toward the sea," he complained.

"There is none shorter," I told him. "This is the only route out of the valley."

"Why are you so certain?"

"I have asked the Indians," I said. "And Father Marcos."

"We should be going to the northeast, not north."

"This is the way that Díaz and Father Marcos and the Moor came. They are the only Spaniards who have been through here. Cíbola lies to the northeast, undoubtedly, yet we reach it by this trail."

I had no suspicion that Mendoza harbored such a thought, but now, looking back, I am sure that at this time he was possessed with the idea of being the first among us to sight the Land of Cíbola. If there had been another way through the cordillera, he would have taken it and left Coronado to arrive at the Seven Cities long after he himself was there.

The stream narrowed before we had gone far and led us into a gorge of gloomy cliffs and thundering water. Here we struggled for two days over stony steeps, suffering many injuries and losing a brace of horses and four pack animals.

On the third day the gorge opened upon a wide, green valley seven or eight leagues in length, where ditches fanned out from a stream to water *milpas* of corn and squash and melons. Soon we came to a village called Popi and were welcomed there with gifts of food, of which we were badly in need.

In the time of the fearsome gorge, there was no chance to work on my map, though I carefully had put down all readings. As soon, therefore, as we encamped, I found a place by the stream and spread my materials on a flat stone.

I was sharpening a quill when Zia came at a run through the meadow. Each day since we had left the Valley of Hearts, whether I clung to a perilous crag or lay in camp too tired to lift a hand, she had asked to know about the map.

As she burst upon me, she asked again. "When do you make it? When?"

"Now."

"A picture of the earthly world?" she asked, using words she had learned from me, "and the seven ocean seas?"

"Only that part of the world we have passed through," I answered. "The Valley of Hearts to the Valley of Sonora."

I opened the portolan and showed her how each page of the book was made of thin reed, and how on these pages sheaths of lamb skin had been glued. I showed her the notes I had taken of the country and the readings made with the cross-staff.

Zia moved from one foot to the other, half listening.

I unwrapped the turkey egg, which I had bartered for at Avipa. I separated the yolk and in a clean place on the stone mixed it with water. Then I dipped quill into yolk and drew a cartouche on the lower right hand corner of the page, the shield of His Majesty, Charles V, enclosed by a fanciful scroll.

"I do not see much," Zia said.

"Now there is not much to see. Later it gets better."

When the egg yolk was dry I carefully glossed it over with soot, gathered from the bottom of a pot.

"Watch closely," I said and passed my hand back and forth like a magician above the design.

Zia held her breath.

"Move closer," I said. "Closer, and keep your eyes open." To make things seem more mysterious, I uttered a few strange words. "Now watch carefully."

With a woolen cloth I then rubbed out the smudge of soot. Suddenly, as if by magic, the shield and scroll stood boldly forth, beautiful to see — white letters and lines on a field of black.

Zia let out her breath, *"Ayee,"* in a cry of delight.

"Once more," she begged me, "make it once more."

"Tomorrow," I said. "Now we do the gorge. We color it ultramarine, which is the most glorious of all blues."

We worked until nightfall, making a fine start on the map, there in the meadow beside the quiet stream. It was good to be away from the uproar of the army, from the talk of gold, which went on night and day, whether we were on the march or resting. Everyone — muleteer and soldier, seamstress and page, amorer and blacksmith, the lowliest and the highest — all soon would have more gold than he could carry, or so each one thought.

When it was too dark to work longer I put the materials away to use in the morning, while Zia washed the brushes and pens in the clear-running stream. But at dawn the trumpet blared and again, like a serpent uncoiling, the army moved on.

# 9

AFTER EIGHT HARD DAYS of fierce suns and short rations, traveling now toward the northeast, we came to Chichilticale, the Red House.

Both Zuñiga and Roa were beside themselves with joy. From Indians at Popi they had heard that Red House was one of the Seven Cities.

"The doors are made of turquoise," Roa told me.

"The women wear belts of gold," Zuñiga said.

"The people have little gold tools," Roa said, "with which to scrape the sweat from their bodies."

"And large golden bowls set with garnets, which they put water in for their animals," Zuñiga said.

"I have talked to Father Marcos," I told them, "and he says that Red House is not one of the cities, though it is a place built by people who once lived in Cíbola. Furthermore, you will see no gold."

My words were of no avail. From the time we left Popi until we reached Red House, for eight days, they talked of the gold that would be found there. They talked with such authority that, despite Father Marcos, many others began to believe them, indeed, most of the army.

"This Marcos," Roa said. "What did he tell us about the Gorge of Sonora?"

"That it was an easy trail for man and beast," Zuñiga replied.

"And what did we encounter?" Roa asked.

"Death at every turn," Zuñiga answered.

"Do you believe that he came here before?" Roa asked.

"No," Zuñiga answered.

"Do you think he is a liar?" Roa asked.

"Yes," said Zuñiga, "the largest."

We came upon Red House suddenly, as we climbed to the crest of a barren hill. It lay below us in a wide, brush-covered arroyo, partly hidden by a grove of ancient trees. Through the foliage I caught glimpses of red walls and paths leading down to them from every direction.

A sigh ran through the army. It grew louder and became a shout of triumph thundering over the hill. Eldorado was finally at hand, the land of turquoise and gold, the first of the Seven Cities.

Our way wound downward to a stream, on a trail long unused. We entered the grove of ancient trees and came upon a wide opening, circular in shape. Before us were the ruins of what once had been a city.

Vast red walls still stood, but the earth-and-timber roofs had collapsed in a mass of rubble. Weeds grew everywhere. Among them lizards scurried and snakes lay coiled. On creaking wings black *zopilotes* soared into the air.

A man and a woman crawled out of the ruins. They were old and toothless, the color of the rubble they had left. In their withered hands they held out to Coronado a gift of dried grubs and grasshoppers.

"Gold," someone shouted. "Where is the gold?"

"Where?" other voices echoed.

The man and woman drew back in bewilderment. But Coronado silenced the soldiers and took the gifts. He then asked about the Sea of Cortés.

"In which direction does it lie?" he asked the old man, Zia translating his words, "and how distant?"

Father Marcos, in his gray robe of Zaragoza cloth, stood listening. "I have been to the Sea of Cortés," he said. "It is only five short leagues from here."

The readings I had made on the coast were with me, as well as the reading I had made that day at noon.

"With all respect to you, Father Marcos," I said, holding out my notes, "I believe the sea to be farther. Perhaps as far as sixty leagues, though I could well be wrong by ten or more."

The old man spoke. "I do not know a sea by that name. But there *is* a sea very far away. When I was a young man I went there to net fish. I was on the trail ten suns going and ten suns returning."

Coronado turned away. His trust in Father Marcos had long since gone, for many of the things Marcos had told him about the trail had proven wrong. The old man's statement, and mine tallied closely. It was dire news. It meant that while the army was traveling toward the northeast, the coast and the Sea of Cortés was trending in the opposite direction, away from us. It meant that he must give up all hope of meeting Alarcón and his ships.

That night men went to parley with Coronado. The fainthearted threatened to turn back. Some wished to strike out for the Sea of Cortés on the chance of finding the ships. Bolder spirits, like Captain Mendoza, wanted to continue on the trail to Cíbola. Some, like Señora Hozes, had no plan yet gave shrill tongue to their anger.

Coronado heard them all. He sat at the door of his tent and listened patiently. He was a man just thirty years old, but in the firelight he looked twice that age.

When the last had spoken, he rose and said in his quiet voice, "You have endured much, and so have earned the right to do what you want. Those who wish to may go in search of Admiral Alarcón or return to your homes. Yet, many or few, the army goes forward. Nor will it stop until it reaches the Land of Cíbola."

Officers and soldiers cheered, but there were some who grumbled. Whereupon Coronado sent for the old man and asked him if he had heard of the Seven Cities.

"In twenty suns," the Indian said, as Zia translated, "you will come to Háwikuh, the first of these." He pointed toward the northeast.

Those who grumbled fell silent. The rest of us moved closer, better to hear Zia, as the old man's words came faint and halting from withered lips.

"In the City of Háwikuh," he said, "there in that city, gold is so common that everyone who uses it is looked down upon."

There was not a whisper from the hundred men and more who pressed around the old man.

"The people of Háwikuh," he said, "possess wash basins of gold but keep them hidden where they cannot be seen. Rather than bathe in them they go and wash in the river. Gold is so common that only the poor eat from gold plates, while the nobles and the king use wooden plates because wood is so rare."

The old man said more, but this was enough to set tongues to wagging. When he had finished and hobbled off to his home in the ruined city, men began to recount the stories they had heard, adding new ones of their own.

I marveled to hear them, at their willingness to believe any tale they heard so long as it dealt with gold. Had not the Indians of Popi lied to them? Were they not on this very night camped beside the ruins of a place that had been described as a thriving city filled with treasure?

There were some, however, who did question the truth of the old man's words. One of these was Captain Mendoza.

When the campfires burned low he summoned Zia and me. Carrying a torch, he led us into the ruins of Red House. There we went from room to room, climbing over piles of rubbish and rotted timber, through narrow halls where rats scurried, into dark places where things of the night squeaked and fluttered, to a room at last that smelled of smoke.

In one corner was a cavelike dwelling, dug into the floor and partly roofed with brush. Into this hole Mendoza thrust his torch. The eyes of the old man stared out at us.

Mendoza gave me the torch and with one hand grasped the Indian by the throat. As if he held something made of faggots and rags, he snatched the old man from the hole and set him on his feet.

Zia put a hand upon Mendoza as if to hold him back. "Do not harm him," she said quietly. Then to the old woman who crouched in the hole squealing like a small animal, she said something that calmed her.

"I will not harm him if he speaks the truth," Mendoza answered. "But tell him that I demand the truth about Háwikuh. Not tales that people wish to hear."

Mendoza took the torch from me and while he waited for Zia to translate, thrust it close to the Indian's face.

"I have spoken with a straight tongue," the old man replied.

"Ask him," said Mendoza, "when it was that he saw the city of Háwikuh."

"I have never seen this city," the Indian said. "But I have spoken to many who have seen it."

"Why have you not seen Háwikuh?" Mendoza demanded. "If this is a place where gold is so abundant, why have you not gone there?"

"For the reason," the Indian said, "that gold means no more to me than to those who live in the city of Háwikuh."

Mendoza raised the torch. I thought for a moment that he was about to strike the old man.

"Tell him that gold means something to me, if not to

him," he said. "Tell him also that if I do not find gold in Háwikuh and in the amounts he has described, I shall come back to this place and cut out the tongue he uses so freely."

Mendoza waited while Zia spoke to the Indian. Then, with a thrust of the torch, he shoved the old man back into the hole.

Next morning when the army marched away from Red House I saw the Indian standing among the shadows of a fallen doorway. As Mendoza rode by the old man glanced out at him and with two crooked fingers made a sign of ill omen.

Whether or not Mendoza saw the sign I do not know. I do know that I saw and many times in the days to come remembered it.

*The Fortress of San Juan de Ulúa*
*Vera Cruz, in New Spain*
*The twenty-seventh day of September*
*The year of our Lord's birth, 1541*

THE WIND BLOWS HOT from the jungle. It tosses the candle flame about but still I can see to write down those things that happened during the first day of my trial.

Two hours after dawn Don Felipe comes to the cell, bringing comb and razor, a fresh doublet which is too small for me, and a word of advice.

"In a short time," he says, "you will stand before the Royal Audiencia. When you face these royal gentlemen, what do you say?"

"I answer the questions asked of me."

"Truthfully?"

"Truthfully."

He snorts through his long, crooked nose. "Then, young señor, you will live here in the Fortress of San Juan for the rest of your days."

"I have wronged the King," I answer bravely, braver than I feel. "But it was not my purpose to do so."

Don Felipe laughs. "Say that as much as you wish. But about the gold, say nothing. Nothing, *señor*. Like your counsel, they care little whether you are guilty or not. What they wish to know is about the treasure. Does

69

it fill the hold of one galleon or perhaps two? Or is it only the size to fill a king's hollow tooth? Where was it found? Where is it hidden? The gentlemen will ask a hundred questions to get the answer to one. Therefore, guard well your tongue."

Before we leave the cell, Don Felipe places a hand on my shoulder. "I think of you always as a son," he says. "When you stand in front of the Royal Audiencia I shall pray for you to the Holy Mother."

I am sure that he will. He wants the treasure for himself.

We climb the stairs together. We pass the sentry box, a sleeping sentry, whom Don Felipe rouses with a kick, and the holes where prisoners are kept.

"One more thing," he says as we cross the esplanade. "One of the judges is as deaf as a stone. Therefore speak up and do not mumble your words."

We reach the chamber of the Royal Audiencia, where two guards stand at the door. Inside I can see nothing, blinded as I am by the sun on the esplanade. Then I make out a small window, which has not been cleaned for months.

In front of the window at a heavy oak table sit three old men who look very much alike, whose faces are the same color as the underside of a sturgeon. They wear well-kempt wigs and black robes trimmed with fur. On their right is the royal fiscal, on their left the fiscal's assistant. The royal notary and two drab-looking clerks sit at another table, near Gamboa, my counsel.

Don Felipe has left me and I stand blinking my eyes.

Then one of the clerks sidles forward, carrying a cross, and halts a step away.

"Do you swear," he says, "to tell the truth before God, the Holy Mary, and the sign of the cross?"

I give my reply in a firm voice and touch the sacred symbol with my right hand, according to the law.

The second clerk rises and begins to read. He runs his words together so that they sound like pebbles falling down a chute. Yet I hear the final accusation.

". . . to defraud and to deceive His Cesarean Majesty, to withhold the King's Royal Fifth, a rightful share of treasure, whose whereabouts is presently unknown, Estéban de Sandoval, a native of the city of Ronda in the Province of Andalucia, and a subject of the true Emperor, stands guilty of a crime against the Crown."

I already know the accusation, but to hear it spoken aloud in the courtroom gives it a different and more serious meaning. Since I have not been asked for my opinion, I say nothing.

The judge then asks if I am to be defended by counsel. Before I can reply, the young lawyer in the shabby doublet is on his feet. He bends forward, making a meek bow which I am certain he has practiced beforehand, and announces that I wish to plead guilty to the charge as read, with one exception.

My plea of "guilty" seems to surprise the royal fiscal, for suddenly he leans forward to whisper to the judges. After a time he slowly rises from behind the black oak table.

He is a squat-faced Spaniard with a protruding lower

lip that reminds me of the King's. He bows to the judge, glances carefully at the window, at the stone walls, at the royal coat of arms, at the stone floor, finally at my boots, the doublet which is too small for me, and the medal which I wear around my neck. He never meets my eyes.

"Your crime," he says, "is great. Are you aware of this?"

I sense that he is laying a trap. "I am aware of the accusation," I answer, "but not of any crime."

He begins to look around the chamber again. "Then you deny that you have deliberately deprived the King of his rightful share of treasure?"

"Yes, sir."

"Do you deny that you found such treasure?"

"Yes."

"Do you deny that a treasure exists?"

In truth, I am forced to answer, "No."

"A treasure exists?"

One of the judges, who has been sitting with his eyes closed, now opens them and looks at me.

"A treasure does exist?" the royal fiscal asks again, raising his voice.

"Yes, sir."

"Treasure exists, but you did not find it?"

"No."

The royal fiscal's glance now has reached the window, but suddenly he looks at me. His eyes are the shape and color of round leaden pellets.

"Since there is a treasure and you did not find it," he

says, "it was therefore found by someone else. Who?"

There is no sound in the chamber except the scratching of a quill.

"Who?" he repeats.

"Captain Blas de Mendoza," I answer.

"Who is this man?"

"He was a member of Coronado's army."

"Captain Mendoza," the royal fiscal says, "found the treasure which you now possess?"

Again, the trap. "The gold," I answer, "is not in my possession."

"Was it ever in your possession?"

Behind me I hear Don Felipe cough. My counsel is gazing at the ragged lace cuffs of his doublet. One of the judges admonishes me to be more prompt with my answers.

The royal fiscal asks his question a second time.

"Yes, it was in my possession," I say.

"When?"

I have to think. "Two months in the past. Perhaps longer."

"How did it come into your possession?"

"Through Captain Mendoza."

"By reason of Captain Mendoza, of course," the fiscal says with a show of irritation. "But how? In what manner?" He leaves the table and walks slowly to where I stand. "Did you steal it?" he asks.

I make no reply, but at once my counsel jumps to his feet. Speaking with an eloquence that surprises me, he objects to what the fiscal has said. He speaks for several minutes and when he is through the three judges nod their heads in agreement.

The royal fiscal strolls to the window and looks out at the sea. He turns around. "Two months ago," he says, "this treasure was in your hands. Of what did it consist?"

"Of gold."

"In what form?"

"In the form of fine dust."

"This gold — where is it?"

I hesitate. I hear someone shuffle his feet. It is likely my jailer, Don Felipe.

"Where?" asks the royal fiscal.

"In the Land of Cíbola," I answer.

"Where in terms of the cross-staff?"

"These terms I do not remember."

"When you hid the gold — and I presume that it is hidden — did you make note of the place?"

"Yes, sir."

"But now you do not remember."

I am aware that I ask the Audiencia to believe something that is unbelievable. Yet I am determined not to confess that I know where the treasure is hidden, if, indeed, I do know.

"I have forgotten," I answer. "The notes are not in my hands."

Behind me Don Felipe clears his throat.

The fiscal says, "I presume that the notes are hidden also, like the gold."

I do not reply.

The fiscal's lead-colored eyes narrow. "Wherever they are, these notes," he says, pausing after each word, "whether they are ten leagues away or a thousand, you shall have them brought here before the Royal Audiencia. And if need be, we shall adjourn the trial until they *are* in this courtroom. For a year, if necessary, or longer."

The fiscal stares straight at me for several moments, as if to allow time for the threat to sink in. Meanwhile, my counsel has risen to his feet and with hand raised is asking for the judges' attention. When it is given, he says something to them, all of which I cannot hear. It concerns the notes, an effort he will make to have them brought before the Audiencia, for the trial is then adjourned until the sixth day of October.

As soon as I am back in my cell, Don Felipe closes the door behind us. He has said nothing on the way. He stands at the door while I light a candle, and smiles. He is the only person I have ever known whose smile makes me uncomfortable.

"I am proud of you," he says. "The way you stood before the Audiencia. It was with great dignity. Like a true gentleman. As if you did not care one *maravedi* whether you were guilty or not."

"I *am* guilty."

"For a certainty, *caballero*. As I have said already. But the guilty I have seen many times. Commonly they pretend to more innocence than those who are innocent. And are quicker to declare it."

He draws closer, within the candle's glow.

"You are now a person of importance," he says. "From

75

this day onward, therefore, until the day you are freed or left to rot, you will be watched. Your every word will be weighed. To the end that the hiding place of the treasure may be found. You will also have visitors — old friends, new friends, persons you have never set eyes upon. Therefore, be cautious with your tongue."

Don Felipe's words are prophetic. He is scarce gone before I am visited by a Captain Martín, commander of the fortress. A round, jovial man, he was not present at the trial, nor at first do I recall having seen him elsewhere. But when he comes into reach of the candle I recognize him from the old days, as a lieutenant in Coronado's army.

Captain Martín accepts my offer of the bench. He speaks of the battle at Háwikuh, in which he was severely wounded, and recalls the morning I set forth from that city with Captain Mendoza.

"How we laughed, *hombre,* to see you go. A girl for a guide, a lame priest, two musicians, an armorer and keeper of horses who could not make a good bodkin. And that madman, Mendoza. Yes, how we laughed. Not to mention you yourself. A stripling who yet could not raise a beard."

We talk for most of an hour about the battle of Háwikuh, but not once does he mention the treasure. Nor when he leaves, though he does say that if there is anything I need he hopes I will inform him of it.

I look forward to his next visit, since he is a freehearted fellow with whom I have shared danger.

The wind still blows hot from the far jungle across

a quiet sea. The star, whose name I do not know, shines brightly. Since the next part of my trial is many days away, I have ample time to write down the events of our journey from Red House to the city of Háwikuh, and of the savage battle which we fought there.

# 10

THE COUNTRY THAT LAY between Red House and Háwikuh was named *Despoblado,* the Uninhabited.

The name was chosen well, for it was a vast wilderness of desert and plain, a land so fierce that at the end of the first day Coronado sent Captain Cárdenas, one of his trusted officers, ahead to explore the way and give warning of dangers. Each day thereafter word came back by messenger of what had been found. The reports were never good, but to know what we would encounter was better than not knowing.

Food had long been scarce. When none was found, save cactus apples and beans from the *mizquitl* bush, we tightened our belts and reduced our rations.

It was the horses that suffered most. At the end of the first week in the *Despoblado,* they began to die, two one day, three the next. Yet, while others grew gaunt or sickened, Mendoza's animals fared well. He ordered Torres to gather grass for the blue roan as we moved ahead, so at night she always had plenty. Her foal actually gained weight. Zia did little except search out tender roots and the young shoots of *mizquitl* and cactus, which she stored in a bag and fed to the foal when we made camp.

When more horses died, Coronado in desperation commanded everyone who was riding to dismount and walk.

Thus on the fourteenth of July we came to a river which ran cold and clear. We crossed it on rafts and suddenly were in a country of heavy timber and grass like that of Castile. Here we grazed our livestock.

The rest gave me a chance to collect the notes I had carefully taken along the way and to begin the map of the *Despoblado*. But after two days Coronado pressed on into the high mountains that rose in front of us, for his army was starving.

Climbing hard we reached the summit and at the eastern edge of a forest a cold spring. As soon as we had encamped, hungry men went in search of berries and roots. Of them, three found a patch of wild parsnips, which they ate. The following day the three died in agony and were buried beside the trail. Their deaths cast a pall upon the army.

That evening horsemen captured three young Indians who were skulking in the trees, and brought them into camp. From them we learned that Háwikuh was only two suns away. But we were told to be cautious, for the Chief of Háwikuh had sworn vengeance upon all Spaniards.

Again Coronado sent Captain Cárdenas and fifteen horsemen ahead. The next afternoon, while we rested on the trail, a rider came galloping toward us, dispatched by Cárdenas with news of an ambush.

"Late yesterday," the rider said, "as we neared a small pass, Indians were sighted on a nearby summit. Captain Cárdenas made signs of peace and, leaving us, went forward with gifts. The Indians came down from the summit and took the gifts and listened respectfully to his words of friendship.

"When they had disappeared," the rider continued, "the Captain posted a mounted guard at the pass and the rest of the men unsaddled. Some hours later, at midnight exactly, a large band of Cíbolans attacked. They made a fearful noise and shot many arrows, which stampeded the horses, leaving most of us on foot. Despite these things, we kept in good order and withstood them. Then the Indians retreated, sounding a little trumpet as they fled."

The army had traveled far that day. We were tired and ready to encamp, but Coronado ordered us forward. We went, aware that it was not because of the ambush. Nor because Háwikuh, the golden city, lay close at hand. At last, after three months and four hundred leagues of marching, the army was down to its final ration — two bushels of corn.

"We reach Háwikuh on the morrow," Coronado told us, "or we starve here on the trail. There is no other choice."

By a half-moon the army traveled late, finished the two last bushels of maize, and while it was still dark marched once more.

We sighted Háwikuh at dawn.

We saw it from afar, through misty air, the sun not

yet risen, across a deserted plain, against sombre red cliffs. The city rose in tiers, many tiers high, each tier stepped back from the one lower, so that it had the shape of a crumpled pyramid.

A hundred shouts went up from the marching column. But Roa said, "I see no gold."

"How could you see gold?" Zuñiga asked. "You do not have the eyes of an eagle. Wait until we draw nearer."

We climbed out of a swale to the plain where the city rested, tier upon tier. We were so close now that dark figures could be seen standing on the parapets. As we drew nearer we heard voices calling, whether in threat or greeting could not be told.

A hush fell over the army. Even Señora Hozes grew quiet. There was no sound except the muffled thud of hooves in the tall grass, the jingle of spurs and hawk bells.

The trill of a small trumpet drifted down the wind and as the sky brightened smoke rose from the topmost tier. A solitary figure held up his hand. Was it in friendship or to warn us away?

We approached a wide space where nothing grew, beaten hard by many feet and criss-crossed by low mounds behind which men might conceal themselves. Here Captain Coronado gave the command to halt.

At that moment the sun rose. It reached the sombre cliffs behind the city. It touched the highest tier of Háwikuh. I watched, holding my breath, while the sun reached lower and lower, until in one burst of radiance the city stood clearly forth.

I saw then that Háwikuh, its walls and parapets, even

in the golden light of morning, were fashioned of mud. They glittered here and there with mica and were a lighter color than the walls of Red House, but they were made of mud, nevertheless.

The gathered army was silent. As I looked at Captain Mendoza who stood beside Coronado, I heard him say, "Perhaps the gold is elsewhere. The old man at Red House said it was hidden from sight."

"Perhaps," Coronado replied in his quiet voice. "We will soon know. But it is food that we need now more than gold."

The army was massed behind him, waiting for the order to attack. There was not a sound on the plain nor in the city of Háwikuh. The parapets were deserted. Smoke no longer rose above the topmost tier.

Suddenly a trumpet called from the direction of the mounds, a distance of a crossbow shot. Before the notes had died away, from behind the mounds, a phalanx of warriors jumped to their feet. They rose as one man, though there were more than two hundred. They stood facing us, armed with arrows and war clubs and protected by round, leather shields.

We were not aware at this moment that news of our coming had spread through the province.

From far-off places warriors had hurried to Háwikuh. All the women and children of the city, and most of the men over sixty, had been sent to a safe place on the high cliffs. Only the braves were left, together with a few old men to counsel them. Nor did we know that hidden within the walls were twice the number that faced us.

The trumpet sounded again. Four of the Indians strode out and marked a line on the earth with corn-meal. At once their comrades began to make hostile gestures, waving shields, brandishing clubs, daring us to cross the line of sacred meal.

Coronado ignored their challenge. He called Captain Cárdenas and five mounted men to his side, also Father Luis, Father Daniel, an interpreter, and Bermejo the notary.

"Tell the Cíbolans," he said, "that we come not to injure them but to defend them, in the name of the great Emperor across the ocean."

Captain Cárdenas advanced with his band and halted short of the line which had been marked, making signs of peace. His men laid down their weapons and he urged the Cíbolans to do likewise. Bermejo the notary then spoke to them for several minutes, but the Indians paid no heed.

Without warning, when Bermejo had finished, a band of Indians rushed forward and began to shoot arrows right and left. One of the shafts pierced his armor, another wounded his horse, a third cut through the skirt of Father Luis' robe. Then, quickly, the Cíbolans drew back.

# 11

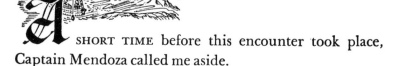

SHORT TIME before this encounter took place, Captain Mendoza called me aside.

"You will need this," he said.

We stood about ten paces behind Coronado, shielded by him and his officers, from the Indians.

Mendoza pushed a matchlock into my hands.

"What do I do with this?" I asked.

"Fool," he said, "you aim it at the Cíbolans and fire."

"But I know nothing about a matchlock," I protested. "I have seen them, but have never used one."

"I will show you. Look closely," he said and instructed me in the way to set the hook, which held the weapon, how to fix the charge and ignite it. "There is nothing to a matchlock," he said. "It is much simpler than an arquebus."

"But I am a cartographer," I said, "not a soldier. I do not wish to shoot anyone."

Mendoza laughed, a laugh without mirth. "You will learn to shoot soon enough," he said. "When you get an arrow against your breastplate, you will suddenly become a soldier. Would you rather be a dead soldier than a live one?"

"Neither," I said, truthfully.

But I took the matchlock, which was now loaded, and a good Toledo blade, which he strapped to my waist.

"Wait here," he said, and went forward to join Coronado.

Beside me were Roa and Zuñiga, also with matchlocks. I still clung to my bundle of maps and materials, so I handed Roa the weapon and ran back to where Zia and Señora Hozes stood under a tree.

"Guard these well," I told Zia.

"I will guard them," she said, and from her voice I knew that she would, with her life if necessary.

I returned and took my place beside Roa and Zuñiga. Holding the matchlock, which reached higher than my head, I waited for a command. I did not feel brave at all. I did not hate the Cíbolans, nor did I wish to shoot at them, but I stood stiffly and looked straight ahead, like a soldier.

Coronado asked for a sack of trinkets, and with four of his officers spurred forward, motioning the rest of us to follow.

He came to the row of earthen mounds and dropped the trinkets. The gifts spread out in front of the Cíbolans, yet they made no move to gather them up. Instead, with clubs raised, they pressed on until they were at the very hooves of Coronado's horse.

The captain-general then spoke to Father Luis, and getting his permission to attack, gave the cry, "Santiago!"

A hush fell over the field. Mendoza raised his sword and shouted, "Death to the Cíbolans!"

The cry was quickly taken up, and as the army marched forward, everyone around me began to chant, "Death to the Cíbolans!"

I stepped out at a brisk pace, the matchlock on my shoulder, but I was cold with fear. I wondered why it was that I, a maker of maps and not a soldier of the King, should be going into battle. With every step my fear increased. I thought of my grandfather who, when he was my age, had fought the Moors at Granada and had been commended for his bravery, yet this did not help. I am not a true Spaniard, I said to myself, for all Spaniards are fearless. Nor did this serve to lessen my fear.

At the first volley the Indians fled. Some scattered across the plain, but most ran to the walls, where their comrades let down ladders and helped them escape within. Behind, they left twenty killed. More would have been killed if Coronado had allowed his horsemen to pursue them.

The fighting, this part of it, was over before I could place my heavy weapon on its hook.

Shortly thereafter, Father Marcos, who was the leader among the priests, came up from the rear. Coronado told him what had happened and that the Cíbolans were barricaded inside the walls.

"Take your shields," Father Marcos said, "and find them."

Coronado first sent his cavalry to surround the city. Before he ordered the charge, however, he again urged the Cíbolans to lay down their weapons. He was answered from the parapets by a shower of arrows.

The shower grew so heavy that the horsemen could not draw near the walls. Crossbowmen and arquebusiers were brought up, but the strings of the bows, which had dried out in the heat of the long march, broke. The arquebusiers arrived so weak from hunger that they could not raise their weapons.

Coronado, deciding to wait no longer, gathered a few men around him and ran toward the walls.

Arrows fell upon the small band, struck breastplate and helmet, yet the men ran on. I watched as they reached the shelter of the walls and one by one slipped through a small opening, into which one of the Indians had crawled.

This secret entrance to Háwikuh, for such it proved to be, was a small hole that only one man could crawl into at a time. The Cíbolans who fled the first volley fired by our soldiers had used the ladders let down to them rather than this opening. Thus its whereabouts would have been unknown to us, except for the Indian who, fleeing for his life, had betrayed it.

Before the last of Coronado's band had disappeared, Mendoza brandished his sword and again shouting, "Death to the Cíbolans!" advanced toward the secret opening.

I was the last to reach it, sent sprawling as I was by a rock thrown from above, which would have killed me had I not worn a helmet. Once there, finding that the matchlock was too cumbersome to handle, I threw it aside.

Blade in hand I crawled through the hole, a dark, winding passageway, filled with a dank and noisome odor. My comrades I could neither see nor hear.

The passage made a sharp turn and began to climb. I crawled over an object, which partly blocked my way, the body of an Indian. I came to a second turning and still another body. Faint light shone ahead of me. Suddenly I was in the sun, on a wide parapet or terrace high above the ground, the roof of the first tier, which was strewn with rocks and spent arrows.

Mendoza and my comrades crouched nearby, against a wall that rose to the second tier of the pyramid. Beyond them stood Coronado and his officers, beside the bodies of several Indians. As I ran for the protection of the wall, two soldiers came along the parapet, dragging a ladder.

Roa pointed above, from whence rocks were raining. "The Cíbolans have escaped us," he said, "but we will follow and slay them one by one."

The soldiers set the ladder against the wall. Brandishing his sword, Coronado beckoned us to follow and began to climb toward the second parapet. He had mounted only half the length of the ladder when I heard the thud of stone upon steel. The sword dropped from Coronado's hand and slowly he fell backwards. His gilded morion rolled to my feet.

He lay stunned for a moment or two, then got to his knees, found his sword, and held it aloft. He was standing with one boot on the ladder, ready to mount again, as a second stone struck him, this time with such force that he slid to the parapet and lay still.

Meanwhile, the Cíbolans shouted in triumph, seeing that our leader had been gravely hurt. And between shouts they made ready to unloose an avalanche of stones upon him.

Stones whistled downward through the air, but in that instant before they struck, both Alvarado and Cárdenas threw themselves across his body. Thus he was saved from further injury. Yet he was close to death, with bad wounds about his head and an arrow deep in his leg.

Soldiers moved him from the parapet and out through the passageway, to where he could be given help, though rocks kept falling and the air was alive with arrows. Cárdenas and Alvarado, vowing death to the Cíbolans, started up the ladder. Our four followed hard on their heels.

I was the last to go, but as I put my foot on the first rung I felt a heavy blow upon my shoulder. Thinking that it had come from above, I reached for the next rung. Then I heard a sound close at hand. I turned. An Indian was crouched at the foot of the ladder. I saw him in time to dodge a second blow which surely would have felled me, for it shattered the rung where I stood.

The Indian stepped back and raised his club. He was young and had a broad face painted with swirls of black and red.

There were two things I could do. I could climb the ladder, for I already had a foot on the second rung. Or leap down upon him, using my sword. One instant the choice was mine, the next instant it was taken from me. With the club still raised, the young Cíbolan, instead of striking again, reached up and grasped my leg.

His grip was hard, as if a trap had sprung shut upon me.

I did not try to wrench myself free, but aimed a blow at his arm. The thrust was quick, yet it missed the mark when he loosed his hold and jumped back. Left suddenly off balance, I pitched forward, with good fortune caught his arm as I fell, and we both went sprawling to the parapet.

He was the first to gain his feet. He had lost his club in the fall and ran to pick it up. In the meantime, on guard with my sword, I rose and circled him until the wall was at my back.

He was older than I, perhaps by a year, and taller. Yet I had the advantage of a helmet and a *cuera* made of thick layers of bull's hide heavily stitched, which covered my body from neck to thigh. His sole protection was a short leather skirt. One advantage was his, however. He was fresh, while I was weak from hunger and the long march.

His back was toward the edge of the parapet. Quickly I moved in with a feint I had learned in camp, thinking to rouse him from his crouch and thus place him for a fatal thrust. The feint was good but as I lunged forward he caught my sword in mid-air with a blow of the club and sent it spinning.

Like a swamp cat, like a *tigreillo*, as the sword left my hand, he was at me. The first blow was glancing. It caught the side of my helmet and slid off, yet I felt it strong. The second blow, which he delivered with all his strength upon my shoulder, made me grind my teeth in pain.

He must have thought that I had not been hurt, that my armor could withstand his blows, for suddenly he dropped the cudgel. Another blow surely would have brought me down.

My sword was some ten paces away. I edged toward it, but before I had covered half the distance the Cíbolan leaped upon me. A hand reached my throat and as it tightened I gave a mighty buffet with my knee. The Indian made a sound deep in his chest. His grip weakened and he bent forward, yet when I aimed another buffet he caught up my leg and we fell together, he on top.

For a while we lay still on the hard earth of the parapet. I was glad of the respite, though my mouth was pressed against the dirt and a dull pain wandered through my skull. From far off came the cries of men, the clash of arms, the wailing of women, a dog barking.

I had lost my helmet in the fall. With one hand — the other I held locked beneath me — the Cíbolan grasped my hair and tried to force my head back. With the strength left to me, I resisted him. His club lay just out of reach. He was quiet for a moment and I knew he was thinking of some way to retrieve it.

The sounds from above grew faint. I could not tell one from another. I was aware only of the blood beating in my head and the sound was like a bell tolling.

The Cíbolan began to writhe, moving little by little

toward the cudgel. The arm I held was smeared with grease, strong and evil-smelling, as was his body.

The cudgel drew closer, but it still was beyond his reach. Suddenly he grasped my hair and again forced my head back. With a quick push he then smashed my face against the earth.

The taste of blood filled my mouth. With it came the thought, and for the first time, that I was struggling with death itself. It was either his life or mine. This knowledge gave me the strength to rise slowly to my knees. At the same moment I loosed his arm and lunged for the club.

It was heavy in my hand. But as he drew himself together and like an animal came toward me on all fours, I brought the club down. He made no outcry when it struck, only the whimper of a hurt child.

Minutes must have passed, perhaps many, I do not know. I was aroused by a voice that came from above. The voice was familiar and I tried to answer, but the words would not come.

Near me lay the young Cíbolan, the cudgel between us.

His eyes were open and in them was no longer the hatred that I had seen before. Behind the swirls of black and red, which only a short time ago had given him the look of a demon, I now saw a young man, scarcely older than I. We could have been friends who had paused to rest beside the road after a long journey.

I heard footsteps and looked up to see Captain Mendoza standing over us. My sword was in his hand.

"Mapmaker Sandoval," he said, "I again come to your aid."

He held out my blade, hilt first.

"Use it," he said.

I raised myself to one knee. My fingers fumbled for the hilt and at last closed around it. Staggering to my feet, I looked down at the Cíbolan. He did not move. He glanced at the bright sword and then at me. In his eyes was neither fear nor hatred nor pleading, only a faint look of puzzlement.

"Strike," Mendoza shouted, "while there is still time."

I could hear him clearly but could think of no words to say. I could not tell him why I stood there with the sword raised and would not use it.

"Death to all Cíbolans!" he cried.

The sword fell to my side, then from my hand. Mendoza picked it up.

"I will teach you to be a soldier," he said, and with one thrust ran the sword through the young Cíbolan.

# 12

I WAS CARRIED from the parapet to a tent outside the walls, where I lay a week or more between life and death. I therefore know nothing of what happened during the rest of the battle, save what I was told.

It seems that Captain Cárdenas took command, after Coronado's injuries, and with great ferocity drove the Indians from one tier to another, higher and higher, until at last they were cornered on the farthest parapet. The Cíbolans then made signs, saying to harm them no more, they wished to leave the city. Cárdenas told them to descend, which they did. They let down ladders and in silence went away to the distant cliffs.

When the last had gone the army broke ranks. It rushed upon the plentiful storehouses, which were filled with maize and beans and turkeys larger than the men had ever seen. More food was eaten that day than on any score of days since the army had left the Valley of Hearts.

After the feast the men slept, feasted again and once more slept. Like terriers they raced through all parts of the city, rooting into bins and the sacred kiva, digging under floors, toppling walls and baking ovens, in search of treasure.

Little was found — no golden basins or portals or paving stones. A few poor trinkets, bits of turquoise, two points of emeralds, and small broken pebbles the color of garnet was everything that the search uncovered.

I was not there to see their disappointment, but it was bitter beyond my power to tell. Mendoza's above all. The first clear sound I heard was his step outside the tent where I lay, six days after the battle. Striding back and forth, he was cursing the old man of Chichilticale.

"On the morrow, as God is my witness," he said, "I shall climb the mountains, cross the *Despoblado,* find that infamous teller of lies, and remove his tongue."

The threat came to naught.

Soon thereafter, when Coronado had sufficiently recovered from his wounds, he asked Mendoza to go with him to a place nearby called Corn Mountain. There they talked with the ruler of the Province and its chiefs. The Cíbolans promised to become subjects of the Spanish King, saying that many moons ago it had been foretold that people like Coronado and his men would come from the south and conquer them.

They also said that to the northwest was a province called Tusayán, where there were seven cities. Surely, they said, these were the cities the Spaniards sought.

Coronado doubted the cacique and his chiefs, but when he told them that the army would camp at Háwikuh the rest of the summer, cities or no cities, they still swore that they were saying the truth.

He told them that men would be sent to seek out this place of Tusayán and return with word of what they found. Did the ruler and the chiefs still speak the truth? Did they wish to change their story of the Seven Cities now, before it was too late?

No, there existed to the northwest a province called Tusayán, a place of many people, of gold and turquoise.

Coronado sent Captain Pedro de Tovar with twenty picked men to look for it. In a different direction he dispatched Captain Cárdenas to find a river where, the cacique said, there lived a nation of giants.

Mendoza could have joined either of these expeditions, but he was jealous of both these officers. Instead, with Roa and Zuñiga, he decided to visit villages nearer at hand, which were said to be like Háwikuh though much smaller, thinking to discover something by chance. If not gold, then he might find turquoise or precious stones.

He had been gone about a week when for the first time I was able to leave my pallet, to sit outside the tent for long hours in the bright summer sun. In another few days I was on my feet, and only because of Zia's care.

From the best spring in Háwikuh she brought me a gourd of cold water thrice each day. If there was a special viand cooking on a fire anywhere in camp, like a haunch of venison, she would manage somehow to bring me a piece of it. She even fetched a barbel fish that Señora Hozes had caught.

"You bring these things," I said, making a joke with her, "so I will become strong enough to work on the map."

She smiled her quick, shy smile. "Because of that

alone," she said. "When is it you begin?"

Montezuma, the aguatil, peered out at me from her pocket.

"Tomorrow," I said.

"You have the strength now."

"This evening," I said, "if you fetch me one of those flavorsome fowls the Cíbolans raise."

"I will bring it."

And she ran off through the camp, to the silvery ringing of the bells that hung from the brim of her corncake hat. Out of breath but within the hour she was back with a plump fowl which we spitted and set to roast over a piñon fire.

The map, with Zia's help, went quickly. When Captain Mendoza returned from the six villages it was complete and we began another.

The men returned without gold or turquoise, but the moment I saw Roa's face, which could not keep a secret, I felt that somewhere among the villages the three had come upon good news. And that whatever the news might be, Mendoza was determined that the rest of the camp would not know about it. My suspicion was soon borne out.

The next morning he left to talk with Coronado. He came back late that afternoon with permission to make a long journey into the northwest.

The following day we spent packing the leather panniers with maize and beans, horseshoes, horseshoe nails, bullet bags, two small casks of gunpowder, lead and firestones, steels and match cords and tools. As gifts to the

Indians we would meet, three panniers were filled with hawk bells, bits of mirror, old gaming cards, trinkets and gauds.

It was only an hour before our departure that Captain Mendoza decided upon a guide. And it was I who changed his mind. He preferred an old man who had gone with him to the six villages, as being more experienced than Zia, and less trouble.

"Maps," I reminded him, "are important to you, or at least that is what you told me when we talked aboard the galleon. In the making of maps on this journey, Zia has been of help."

"In what way?" he asked. "Tell me of one."

"In the mixing of colors. The cleaning of brushes. The gathering of soot, which is necessary but not pleasant. She even can draw a map by herself. A small one."

He was surprised at this, but not convinced. "She is a girl," he said. "We are starting on a long journey."

"She has just finished a long journey," I said, "and in better health and spirits than any of us, except Father Francisco. Recall that Cortés, conqueror of Mexico, was guided by a girl. By Marina, without whom he would have been lost. Who not alone guided him but also won him friends among hostile Indians."

It was this last argument which, I think, weighed with him the most, for he held Cortés in high esteem.

On the morning we left, Zia came to my tent with a gift of farewell. She handed me a deerskin case, soft and beautifully sewn.

"This is for your maps and paints," she said. "And for the thing you look at the sun with."

There was sadness in her eyes, but she tried to smile. I thanked her and said, "Do you wish to go with us?"

She tried to speak.

"Then go and talk to Captain Mendoza," I told her. "He wants you to come. He thinks you are the best guide in all of New Spain."

Without a word, she ran skipping and jumping toward the Captain's tent.

At noon we rode out from Háwikuh.

The sun shone on helmets and breastplates. Roa beat on his drum and Zuñiga played his flute. Torres carried a yellow pennon that fluttered in the wind. Father Francisco carried his small wooden cross. Hooves and tinkling hawk bells made a merry sound.

In the lead on the blue roan rode Captain Mendoza. He sat erect in his high, Spanish saddle, elegant in scarlet doublet and buff-colored jackboots, shining cuirass and gilded morion. At his heels trotted Tigre, the big gray dog, which he had bought for a peso.

Zia walked behind him, not minding the dust, as close to the foal as she could. I wondered whether it was the colors we would magically mix and the maps we would draw from them, or this black little beast that had lured her to go with us, when well she might have remained with Coronado, the great Captain-General. It was neither one nor the other, as I was to learn, but late.

Zuñiga, Roa and I rode next. Father Francisco and

Torres brought up the rear, Torres leading four good horses and eight sturdy mules.

We passed through the crowded camp. Señora Hozes again put her fingers in her ears at the sounds our musicians drew from drum and flute. Watchers wished us good fortune. One or two gave tongue to unseemly taunts.

The taunts did not disturb me. Tied to my saddle, in the deerskin case Zia had made for me, were my maps, supplies, and cross-staff. The sound of rowel and bell and hoofbeat quickened my blood. Far off rose mysterious mountains, watching over a land no map maker had yet set eyes upon. Already a map began to take shape in my mind. It would be the first map ever drawn of Háwikuh and this country to the north, one which the printers of Seville and Madrid would marvel at.

"It will be black and gold," I shouted to Zia. "With a red windrose."

She knew what I meant. "A beautiful one," she called back.

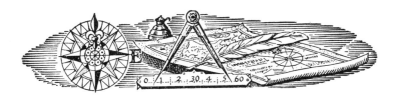

*The Fortress of San Juan de Ulúa*
*Vera Cruz, in New Spain*
*The sixth day of October*
*The year of our Lord's birth, 1541*

COUNSEL GAMBOA comes to my cell early in the morning, his third visit in as many days, and his fourth since the last session of the trial. At that time we decided to give the notes, when they arrived from Mexico City, to the Audiencia. My decision to do so was based on the belief that no one, even a skilled cartographer, could make head or tail of them.

"They have not come," I tell him, "though Don Felipe expects them today or tomorrow."

Counsel Gamboa looks more frayed than usual. I hope that from this trial, which must be his first, he will gain a reputation and some ducats.

"It would be better today," he says. "But I can explain."

"With the notes, what will be my sentence?" I ask him. This has been much on my mind.

Gamboa is thinking and it takes him time to reply. "Five years, possibly."

"Without them?"

"As I said before, it could be as much as fifteen years.

As little as ten. But here in San Juan ten would be like fifty years elsewhere."

"Yes, you have told me this," I answer. "I had forgotten."

We climb the stairs together, Don Felipe at our heels, and cross the esplanade. Before we reach the courtroom, Counsel Gamboa says, "If the royal fiscal asks you to describe the size of the treasure — in all likelihood he will not, for an excellent reason, but if he does — what do you plan to say?"

"The truth, as I remember it."

Under his breath, Counsel Gamboa says, "What is the truth?"

I am about to reply, but we have reached the door of the courtroom, and as I begin, Don Felipe steps between us and gives me a gentle shove through the doorway.

The courtroom is filled with a throng of the curious. They stand three rows deep around two sides and the back of the room. It is very hot. The three judges sit with their robes pulled up to their knees, to catch what air there is. In their black robes trimmed with fur, and their wigs which are worn well back from their foreheads, they remind me of the three black *zopilotes* perched on the ruined walls of Red House, the morning we marched away to Háwikuh. It is not a good omen.

I am shown to a bench and there I sit for a long time while Counsel Gamboa talks to the royal fiscal. The fiscal seems to be in a pleasant mood, for he smiles now and then, and once even laughs. Again I am called to swear upon the cross, which I solemnly do.

The first question surprises me.

"This hoard of gold," the fiscal says, "which you have hidden, and by so doing have defrauded the King of his royal fifth, this treasure is of what size?"

"It was never weighed," I answer.

"Gold is heavy," he says. "How was it carried?"

"By pack train."

"Horses?"

"Horses and mules."

"How many of each?"

"Eight mules and four horses."

"Twelve animals carried how many pounds?"

"I do not know."

"How many pounds does one animal carry?"

"A horse, two hundred. A mule, three hundred."

"Each animal was loaded with all the gold it could carry?"

"Yes, sir."

The lips of the royal fiscal move soundlessly, adding figures in his head. Everyone at the table is adding figures, as well as my counsel. The clerks use their quills. I am certain that Don Felipe, standing quietly behind me, is adding figures — everyone in the chamber, for that matter, even the three judges.

"The treasure train," the fiscal says at last, "consisted of some sixty thousand *onzas* of gold?"

Silence falls upon the courtroom. It is so quiet I hear the breaking of waves against the fortress walls. Everyone is now changing *onzas* into gold *castellanos* or double doubloons.

The royal fiscal repeats his question.

"The gold was never weighed," I answer.

"But if it had been weighed, the amount would approach the sum of sixty thousand *onzas?*"

"More, sir, or less."

The fiscal walks to a table and drinks from a small pitcher.

"You have testified," he says, "that this treasure was in the form of fine dust. How was it contained?"

"In leather bags."

"And when you hid the treasure, it was of course in the leather bags?"

"Yes, sir."

"And where you hid the gold, the place, is shown in the notes which will be presented to the Royal Audiencia?"

"Yes, sir."

"Who was with you when the treasure was hidden?" the fiscal asks.

"I was alone."

"How many were in the party before the gold was hidden?"

I name them one by one, beginning with Captain Mendoza.

"There were five, including yourself?"

"Yes, sir."

The royal fiscal turns his back, walks to where the three judges are seated, and talks to them in a low voice, about what I do not know. When he again faces me, after a long interval, he asks me only a few questions and the session ends. The questions are so foolish that I have forgotten them, though they may turn up later to my discomfort, you never can be certain.

Back in my cell, Don Felipe looks at me in silence. At last he says, speaking with difficulty, "Sixty thousand *onzas*. Of gold! Think of it!"

I say nothing and suddenly, struck by suspicion, he draws near and thrusts out his cudgel-like chin.

"You spoke the truth to the Royal Audiencia?" he demands. "The hoard is of that enormity? Twelve animals were needed to transport it? Sixty thousand gold *onzas?*"

"The truth," I answer.

This does not satisfy him.

"There are prisoners," he says, "who have confessed to crimes, heinous ones, which they did not commit. They have confessed simply because they thought to gain importance in the eyes of the world."

From his neck he takes a silver cross and holds it out to me.

"Swear before Mary, the Virgin, that you have spoken the truth."

This I do, to his satisfaction. Yet there is still something that worries him. He strides up and down the cell, three steps forward, three steps back. The cell is too small to stride in. I wonder if he himself has ever been imprisoned in this fortress, for the walking back and forth is the mark of one who was once a prisoner.

"The notes will arrive today," he says, "today or tomorrow. When they do, they will be given to me. By the messenger whom I sent, who is in my pay. They will be given to me first, not to the Royal Audiencia. I will then give them to you and from them you will draw the map of Cíbola, the hiding place of the treasure. When this is done, and only then, will I release them to the Audiencia. Do you understand?"

I nod, though determined that the map shall be no more complete than the notes from which it is drawn.

The hour is now too late for visitors. My quill is sharp and I have a new supply of paper, thanks to Don Felipe. Beyond the barred window the star glows in the west. The trial continues tomorrow, whether the notes arrive or not. But perhaps I will have time to write down the details of our journey to Nexpan, City of the Abyss, and of the stream we found there, which was strewn with gold.

# 13

TWELVE DAYS FROM HÁWIKUH, the last day through heavy stands of pine and spruce, we came near evening to a break in the forest. In the distance rose a series of cliffs, at the same height we were traveling, scarlet-tinted and oddly shaped, like spires, terraced walls, and battlements.

Captain Mendoza reined in his horse. *"Hola!"* he shouted, "the scarlet cliffs!"

He need not have shouted, for we all saw. Throughout the day, every league we traveled, we had looked for the scarlet cliffs, the sign that marked the location of Nexpan, City of the Abyss. Or so Captain Mendoza had been told by the cacique of the sixth village of the six villages near Háwikuh.

At the foot of the cliffs, the chieftain had said, wound a mighty river. And near the river, at a place marked by three pinnacles (here, according to Roa, the chieftain had made three marks on the ground) was a large city, which could be reached by following a stream that ran into the river.

The chieftain said nothing about the presence of gold in the city. It was for this reason that Mendoza believed him, this alone, and decided to make the journey.

"Where is the river?" Zuñiga asked.

"Below the cliffs," said Torres. "Where you cannot see it."

"What if there is no river?" Zuñiga asked.

"Or no city," Roa said.

"Then we return to Háwikuh," I answered.

"Though we find the city," Roa said, "will it not be another like Red House?"

"Or like Háwikuh," Zuñiga said. "Where we fight with few against many."

Father Francisco, gathering things among the trees, said nothing. Nor did Mendoza, but he led us on toward the scarlet cliffs where the last light hung.

The cliffs retreated, or seemed to, then the light died and darkness gathered among the trees. As we were about to halt for the night, a small wind sprang up. It smelled not of pines but of *mizquitl* bushes and open spaces.

My horse pricked up its ears, and at the head of the column, Mendoza's roan suddenly neighed. It was a warning, a sound of fear, which chilled my blood and brought us all to a halt.

I sprang to the ground but held onto the reins. Fighting the heavy Spanish bit, the roan neighed again. Father Francisco hobbled past me in the darkness and I followed, leaving my horse. I came to a flat place, a rock ledge. The sky was lighter than the earth and against it I saw Francisco standing with arms outstretched.

"A chasm," he cried, "an abyss bigger than half the world."

I groped my way to him across the ledge. Below us lay blackness, fold upon fold, deep and endless. From it a warm breeze welled upward, as if the earth itself were breathing.

The others came and stood beside us. Roa found a stone, which he threw out into the darkness, and we waited for it to strike. Second followed second and we heard nothing. Then, far and faint, a sound, a rustle like a leaf falling, drifted up from below.

"Holy Mother," someone whispered.

One by one we silently crept back into the trees, away from the Abyss. We tethered the animals and ate supper and lay down, but few of us slept. At daybreak we went to the ledge where we had stood the night before.

There we found a rampart of rock, shaped like a great sickle. Below its rim, as if sheared off in one mighty stroke, the rampart fell downward for more than a league. At its foot was a wide bench covered with stones that had fallen from above. A pine which grew there seemed no larger than a bush. Many leagues away, at the eastern boundaries of the Abyss, stood the scarlet cliffs we had seen at dusk.

For a long time, no one spoke. Then Mendoza raised his sword, claiming all that lay before us in the name of His Cesarean Majesty, Charles the Fifth. Father Francisco planted the cross and we knelt beside it and thanked God who at the last moment had snatched us back from death.

Yet, for all our good fortune, we were faced with a hard decision.

Should we go northward, along the rampart, or to the south, hoping to find a way into the Abyss? In both directions the rampart curved away beyond sight. Should we turn back and retrace our steps to Háwikuh? Our first amazement gone, our thankfulness forgotten, we stood beside the cross and lamented our fate.

Mendoza said, "The chieftain is a liar of great proportions. May he roast in hell."

"Indians everywhere are liars," Roa said, "from the Province of Panamá to Háwikuh."

"May they roast in the fires," Zuñiga said.

"But the scarlet cliffs are there," Father Francisco replied, "as the chieftain said."

"So is the Abyss," Mendoza answered, "of which he did not speak. And where, dear Father, is the river which he did speak of?"

Zia had left us to wander along the rampart. As she stopped to toss a rock into the air, I heard her call. She was always finding something that interested her but no one else, so she called again before I went to where she stood, hopping from one foot to the other.

"Look," she said and pointed toward the bottom of the Abyss. "There, by the small hill of yellow stone."

I looked, saw the hill, and nothing else.

She pulled my head down. "Look where I point."

I looked again, grew dizzy with looking, but at last made out a strip of green. "Grass," I said and turned away.

110

"Not grass," she cried, pulling me back. "See, it is water. Water that runs. A river!"

I looked anew and found the hill of yellow stone, the strip of green no larger than my hand. I saw that it was not grass but a bend of shore, and on both sides of it was white sand.

"Do you see?"

"Yes," I said.

"A river?"

"A river," I said, "a mighty one."

# 14

WE SPENT A DAY in search of a path into the Abyss. Forming two parties, Mendoza sent one south along the rampart, the other to the north, in the hope that if there were a city beside the river its people would have a trail by which to go up and down.

No trail was found nor footprints, save those of deer and mountain lion. But we did find a shallow crevice, overgrown by wind-bent pine, that wound downward along the stony face of the rampart. This we decided to try, there being no other choice.

The animals, including the big gray dog, were left in the care of Torres. Food was taken for eight days.

"If we are not back by the eighth day," Captain Mendoza said, "return to Háwikuh for help."

"While you are gone," Torres replied, "I will search for a better path to the river."

"Remain here and search for nothing," Mendoza said. "If time grows heavy, spend it on Tigre. He progresses, but he is still more lamb than tiger."

"You will not know him when you return," Torres said.

Experience gained in the fearsome Gorge of Sonora helped us greatly. Before the sun was a lance high, we had descended deep along the crevice, scrambling from one tree to another. This crevice led to a second, then to a ledge from which we could see the cross and Torres waving from the rampart.

By a series of such crevices, which were like steep ladders, we reached a bench covered with bushes, heavy with berries bitter to the taste.

It was now afternoon and since clouds hid the sky and portended rain, we made camp. From branches and brush we made a good shelter and were safe within before the first thunder rolled.

Rain fell until dusk. Around us water ran, hanging from the ramparts above in silver threads. The sky cleared and through the clear air we saw a different stretch of the river. It was off to the south, but so far below that it looked like the coils of a green serpent.

By nightfall we had explored the bench, finding that on two sides it was an unbroken scarp. To the east, however, the rock had broken away and formed a fan-shaped slope. At dawn, with much difficulty, we descended this slope and came to a second bench.

Here there were no pines, only sparse-leaved bush, similar to those in the Valley of Hearts. Here Zia found a shell, half buried in the earth, the size of my fist and fluted. It was like those she had picked up around the lagoon on the Sea of Cortés. It puzzled me how a shell could be in this place, so far from the sea. And it puzzles me still.

Next afternoon, having traveled the morning down a tortuous steep, we came to sand dunes and the river.

The river was about two hundred paces in width and ran faster than a man can walk. Gray rocks broke its surface and below the surface unseen rocks were marked by whirlpools and white water. The sound of its running was like the groans of a thousand demons.

"We can never reach the far bank," said Roa.

"Nor do we need to," Mendoza answered. "Unless the city lies there."

"If it does, then we will never see it," Roa said.

"If it does, having come this far, we shall," said Mendoza.

"God be with us," said Zuñiga.

Southward the river ran between high bastions, but to the north were stretches of beach. Setting out toward them, we had gone for an hour when fog overtook us. Since we could not see farther than a few steps, we made a fire and camped.

"What I wish to know," Roa said, standing beside the burning driftwood, "is how we carry gold back to the mules."

Looking up at the ramparts we had left almost two days before, a thin line nearly lost in the sky, I wondered also.

"We carry it on our backs, of course," Mendoza said. "One *arroba* to the man. More, if need be."

"I have much trouble carrying myself," said Father Francisco.

"If we die, as we may," said Zuñiga, who often spoke

foolishly, "we will become angels. Then we can fly straight up with the gold."

"Angels," said Father Francisco, "have no use for gold." He turned to Mendoza. "How does a man carry one *arroba* of gold back along the way we have come?"

"Gold," Mendoza said, "can be very light. The lightest burden of all."

The first stars came out. It is said that stars seem brighter when seen from the bottom of a well. Of this, I do not know. I do know that these were as bright as wondrous jewels.

With night a wind rose and blew along the river. It carried a smell, faint yet familiar.

"Indian fires," Zia said. *"Mizquitl wood."*

Mendoza jumped to his feet and shouted.

His voice was drowned in the roar of the river. It made no difference. The Indians of Nexpan already had seen us.

It was still dark beside the river as dawn broke, but above us light swept the bastion's rim. There, like figures of burnished copper, stood three men. They were too far away to hear us so we waved, beckoning them to descend. In answer they pointed down river and vanished.

It was a moment of excitement. The chieftain, for all our doubts, had spoken the truth. We had found the scarlet cliffs, the mighty river he had described. The Indians proved that a city lay near at hand. It was a moment of caution also, for Háwikuh we still remembered.

We did not wait to eat but set off down the river, singing.  Our only lack was music — drum and flute having been left behind.  Within the hour we sighted three spires on the far side of the river, and at the same time, a place where the bastion was cleft.

The cleft was not much wider than my outstretched arms.  Its sides towered straight toward the sky, black as a raven's wing.  Through it coursed a swift stream which flowed into the river over black, gleaming stones.  Beside the stream was a path worn by many feet.

This path we took and once inside the cleft found ourselves in half-darkness.  Giant ferns that grew along the stream dripped water, and cold mist wet our faces.  The stone path was slippery underfoot.

Soon the defile narrowed and closed over our heads.  We could only find our way by touching the dank walls.  The stream thundered beside us, as we scrambled along in utter darkness.  Abruptly we came into sunlight.

Before us lay a vast meadow, more than a league in breadth and in width, enclosed on all sides by high, rock bastions, like those that enclosed the river.  Through it wandered the stream we had followed and along the banks grew cottonwood and willow and ripening berries.  Brown, wheatlike grass stretched away to the far bastions like a placid lake, broken only by islets of grazing deer and mountain sheep.

Speechless, I stared at the peaceful world that lay before me.

"Paradise," Father Francisco said, "must have looked like this on the first day."

"But where," said Mendoza, "lies the city?"

I pointed to a blue cloud above a distant field.

"Smoke," Mendoza said, "but not house or hut."

He set the matchlock and fired. Deer foraging nearby raised their heads and looked at us curiously.

"That will bring someone," Mendoza said.

Before the echo of the blast died away, an Indian rose up from behind a tree and came to where we stood and touched his forehead to the earth.

He said nothing in reply to Zia's questions, of which there were many. Nor did he show surprise at the deafening blast. Nor at the object that caused it. Nor at our strange presence. He looked at each of us in turn, out of eyes that were like the eyes of a lizard, then he started up the stream, motioning us to follow.

Zia said, "He understands nothing of what I asked. I used three languages and still he did not understand. We shall have much trouble, I fear."

"Without words," Mendoza said, "we shall have less trouble. With signs there is no loose talk."

"You do not wish me to talk?" Zia said.

Mendoza smiled, a rare thing with him. "Talk, if it pleases you. I will not listen."

"It does not please me much to talk," Zia said. "It would please me more to sit on a saddle. The same as you do. On the back of the blue roan's daughter. And say no words while I am there. No words, in any language."

"The daughter is too young to ride," Mendoza said.

"When will she not be too young?"

"Soon," he said.

"Then I can sit on her?"

Mendoza did not answer.

"Already I have a name for her," Zia said. "It is Blue Star."

Mendoza no longer was listening. From his pack he had taken a round, silver badge, the size of a small platter and polished to reflect the sun. A silver chain was fastened to it and this he hung around his neck.

When we reached the far end of the meadow where the fires burned a crowd of men and women moved toward us out of the trees. Mendoza held up the badge so that the sun struck it and threw back a flash of light into their faces. Most Indians were worshipers of the sun, and he had devised the badge to thus impress them.

The Indians stopped as the light blinded their eyes. Except for a tall man, who kept on toward us. He was not young yet he was strongly proportioned, the true color of copper, and walked lightly on his feet like an animal. When he reached us he did not touch his forehead to the earth, as had the first Indian.

Captain Mendoza said, "I am the Son of the Sun. Likewise an emissary of the noblest of Kings, and of Christ, Lord of the World."

Zia changed his words into the dialect she had used at Háwikuh, but the Indian shook his head. She tried three other dialects before he nodded and said that his name was Quantah and that he was the cacique of Nexpan.

Mendoza bowed low, then gave him a string of bright beads and two small pieces of mirror. "Ask," he said to Zia, "where the city is which he rules."

118

To this Chief Quantah answered with a proud sweep of a hand and one brief sentence.

"The sky, the clouds," Zia said, "the high bastions, the stream, the *milpas* and meadows, the beasts that graze among them, are the city he rules."

Mendoza took a long breath. "Ask him then where his people live."

Chief Quantah pointed to a grove of cottonwoods.

Zia said, "His people live among the trees. They have no need of houses because here the sun shines always."

"If they have no need of houses," Mendoza said, "then they have no need of gold. But ask him."

Zia spoke to the chief. He shook his head.

"Show him this," Mendoza said, taking a gold medallion from his neck.

Chief Quantah still shook his head. He was glancing at the matchlock which Zuñiga held. He now wished to know if it were this that made the noise of thunder.

Seizing the weapon, Mendoza set it, aimed at the trunk of a young cottonwood some twenty paces away, and fired. Smoke billowed. The cottonwood swayed and crashed at Chief Quantah's feet.

"Now ask him if he has gold," Mendoza said. "The matchlock may have improved his memory."

Quantah looked at the tree with mild surprise, then at the weapon, but said nothing more. And when Zia asked him again about gold, again he shook his head.

# 15

WE ATE THAT EVENING among the trees, from mats heaped high with food we had not seen since long before in Avipa.

During the meal a band of young braves danced and two old men plucked thin tunes from gourdlike drums. Mendoza ate little, and I doubt that he saw the dancing or heard the music. Later, after we were shown a place to camp beside a stand of willows, he left us and hurried off toward the stream.

The night was warm and a half moon shone, so we did not build a fire, but stretched out in the deep, sweet-smelling grass. From long custom on the trail I put my sword within reach.

Roa laughed. "What is it that you fear? Snakes? Wild animals? Surely not the Indians of Nexpan, who have no weapons."

"They may possess stones," I said, "like the ones at Háwikuh."

Roa had come through the battle unscathed by stone, arrow or club. He was shaped like a barrel, a good oaken cask from Jerez de la Frontera, and even the march from

Cortés' Sea had not lessened his girth. He was the only fat Spaniard I have ever known.

"If they do have stones," he said, "they will not use them. Not if they remember the matchlock. How one shot sent the tree crashing down."

"The business of the tree," Father Francisco said, "I did not like. It was not an act of friendship."

"Indians know nothing of friendship," Roa said.

"The matchlock speaks louder than pious words," Zuñiga said.

"It speaks a language which I do not understand," Father Francisco answered.

The three went on, and as I lay there and half-listened while the moon wheeled down the sky, I was overcome with foreboding. This is the beginning of trouble between Father Francisco and the others, I thought. And I was right, thinking it. In the days to come trouble lay in store for them, for us all.

The moon dropped behind the bastions. From the dark sky stars sprang forth. It was deep in the night and I heard Captain Mendoza coming through the meadow. The rest were asleep. I raised myself on an elbow. He knelt beside me and put his hand on my shoulder.

"When we came up the stream at dusk," he said, "I thought that I saw bright glints in the water. In the sand on the bed of the stream. Now, by the moon's light, I have seen them again." He paused, his hand was trembling. "As God is my witness, it is gold I saw. The stream carries gold!"

Mendoza must have slept little that night, for whenever

I was awake I heard him pacing. With the first gray light he roused the camp.

"Gold," he shouted. "Bring your helmets and fill them with gold."

Roa and Zuñiga, on their feet in an instant, found their helmets and stumbled off after Mendoza, who had already reached the stream.

Zia was still asleep and Father Francisco pretended to be. As for myself, I settled back into the fragrant grass and thought about the journey from Háwikuh to the ramparts of the Abyss, of the mountains we had crossed, the streams and mesas, of the notes I faithfully had put down in my journal and the map I would make from them. As I rose and went to bathe, the map was clear in my mind — its size, its colors, the Lullian nocturnal, everything. It would be the finest map I had ever limned.

In the gray light I saw the three men wading along the stream, about a furlong below me. They would stop and bend over, raise up, put their heads together, then slowly move on. They looked like three herons fishing.

The sun had not risen, yet on the stream's sandy bottom I made out an object, a dull glow of metal. I reached down and grasped it. It was the size and shape of a chestnut, a large chestnut, rough to the touch, covered with dark pocks and crevices, and very heavy. There was no mistaking it.

For months, wherever men gathered, I had heard little except the talk of gold. In the taverns of Mexico City, on shipboard or on the trail, even in the streets of Seville when I first came to that city to take up my studies, it was on everyone's tongue. Yet never before had I held a piece of the metal in my hand. Nor seen it, save after it had been fashioned into medallions or the King's *castellanos*.

The nugget lay heavy in my palm. I turned it over, examining all its sides, the sharp edges, the pocks, the crevices. To be certain, I put it between my teeth and bit down. With strange elation I saw that I had left a mark upon it. This was the test Mendoza had once described to me.

I looked at the nugget, at two others lying on the stream bed nearby, and a curious feeling seized me, which I cannot explain. It was like a fever and a sickness. It was as if all the stories of gold that men had told me, all their dreams of power and wealth, had suddenly come alive in my own blood.

"In a short time," I said to myself, "I can fill my helmet. I will search the stream and fill many helmets. Tomorrow is soon enough to work on the map."

While I stood and gazed at the nugget, feeling its massy pull against my hand, a boy came with a message from Chief Quantah. But for this I would have stayed there on the stream all day, searching the sandy bed for gold.

# 16

THE BOY SHOWED the way to a place beyond the cottonwood grove.

Here in a grassy swale the people of Nexpan were gathered. They knelt in a half-circle below a stone altar festooned with greenery and wild flowers. On the altar stood Chief Quantah, his arms held out toward the sun which had not yet risen. Everyone was silent. Every face was turned to the east and the dark stone bastion.

Zia knelt beside me in the grass. I had thought to kneel also, but Father Francisco nudged my arm.

A thread of light showed along the bastion's rim. A murmur ran through the throng. The thread widened. The bastion was suddenly ablaze and the murmur swelled to a chant. It was a cry of wonder and delight, as if the sun had never risen before.

The worshipers fell silent and the cacique spoke three words slowly, three times over. After he had finished, the people went singing to the grove, where pyramids of fruit were already set out, and gourds filled with a custard made of sheep's milk and piñon nuts.

Quantah asked us, as we sat on the grass, about our leader. With Zia's help Father Francisco told him that

Mendoza had gone to search for gold. The chief shook his head.

"This gold," he said, "why is it of such value that a man goes hungry to search for it?"

"Gold," Father Francisco replied, "can be traded for gold *castellanos*. If a man has many *castellanos*, he can buy many things. If he can buy many things, he is a *rico*, a person of wealth and of power over others."

Chief Quantah nodded, but I doubt that he understood what was said. Though later he did understand much of Father Francisco's little sermon.

During the time when we had waited for the sun to rise, Father Francisco had held the cross in front of him. He held it as a shield against the pagan sun, the kneeling figures and the worshipful chant. On his face was a look just as intense as the look of Captain Mendoza when he had left that morning to hunt for gold.

After we had eaten, Father Francisco took the cross and led Quantah to the stone altar. Among the boughs and flowers he planted the cross, which was taller than he and made from a cottonwood branch.

He then told in simple words, as Zia changed them into Quantah's language, the story of Christ, the Son of God. How He had lived and how He had died on a cross like the one there before us.

Chief Quantah listened and from time to time nodded his head, saying that he understood.

Then Father Francisco told how when Christ died on the cross, at that moment, at midday with the sun shining, how the sky grew dark and the earth moved and the hill where the cross stood was rent asunder. He told how they buried Christ in a tomb hewn out of the rock and in front of it rolled a large stone.

Chief Quantah looked at the sun and afterwards at the cross, which he touched with his hand.

"On the third day after Christ was buried," Father Francisco said, "as the sun rose on that day, the watchers saw that the stone had been rolled back from the tomb and that the tomb was empty."

Quantah said, "Who was it that took the man from the tomb in the rock?"

"He was not taken away by anyone," Father Francisco said. "The rock fell apart and He rose from the dead."

Quantah asked Zia to repeat these last words. When she did he said, "I understand the death and the darkening sky and the tomb. But I do not understand how a dead man rises."

Father Francisco was silent, too puzzled to know what more to say.

A bee was seeking honey in one of the flowers, and seeing it, he reached down and caught it up. He asked for a gourd of water, and when it was brought, he held the bee under the water until it grew still, then set it on a rock.

A limp ball of fuzz and gauzy wings, it seemed dead. But slowly, as the sun's heat dried it off, the bee began to stir, to move one wing and then the other. Suddenly it rose on its legs and flew away.

Chief Quantah made a gesture toward the sky. "This man who was dead and then was alive and then flew away, I would like to talk with."

"Any day or any night you can talk to Him," Father Francisco said. "We can talk to Him now."

He took Chief Quantah's hand, the two men knelt beside the cross, and Father Francisco prayed.

The prayer over, Quantah said, "I heard you speak to Him, but though I listened carefully I did not hear Him speak to you."

"When you yourself pray," Father Francisco said, "then you will hear Him."

"Will He speak in the language of Nexpan?" Quantah asked.

"He speaks in many languages," Father Francisco said. "In all the languages spoken by men."

Chief Quantah said, "I would like to know more about this man. When He went through the land, before He was slain, what did He say to people?"

"Love one another, this is what He said," Father Francisco answered. "He told the people many things, but what He told them mostly was this — Love one another."

We left the cross standing on the altar. As we neared the grove the three men ran out of the trees, clasping their helmets. When we gathered round they held them up for us to see. In the bottom of each was a handful of gold — bright nuggets the size of a pea and larger.

Chief Quantah took one of the nuggets from Mendoza's helmet. "I have seen these things before," he said. "Our stream has many." He dropped the gold, as if it were of no value, and pointed to the north. "Near the city of Tawhi, there is a stream that flows into our stream. It has many such bright pebbles. Many more than we have. But gather what you wish."

"There are few pebbles here," Mendoza said. "Most of the gold is in the form of dust, which is too small to gather."

"And the water is too cold," Roa said. "It chills the bones."

Wet to the waist, teeth chattering, the three men looked frozen.

"We need a dozen fleece," Mendoza said.

"The sheep already have been shorn and the wool combed," Chief Quantah said. "Why do you need the fleece?"

Mendoza told him that it was a way of gathering gold, that fleece were anchored in the stream and, as the water flowed over them, dust and flakes clung to the wool.

"I would like to see this," Quantah said, "but I have no fleece."

"We can use hides instead."

"I have no hides."

"Then," said Mendoza, drawing from his doublet a gaming card, a dog-eared *rey* of swords, "I pay you for a dozen slaughtered sheep."

Quantah refused the card. "In Nexpan," he said, "sheep are not slaughtered for their hides. Nor for any reason."

"Hundreds of sheep graze your pastures," Mendoza said. "What do you wish, two cards?"

"None."

Quantah then gave a long speech. All Zia translated was that among the people of Nexpan it was a crime to kill sheep and those who did were banished from the city.

Mendoza stood staring into his helmet at the pile of bright gold.

Little did the cacique know that he was speaking to a man who had journeyed thousands of leagues across seas and mountains and deserts, who had faced thirst and starvation, death itself, all for the gold which now lay close.

I feared that by some rash word or act Mendoza would make us enemies in the city. But he said nothing more about the fleece, and with Roa and Zuñiga went off toward the camp.

As I watched them go I was suddenly aware that I gripped something in my hand. It was the gold nugget, which I still held. I kept my fingers tightly closed and did not show it.

"The nugget is larger than any that Mendoza or Zuñiga or Roa dug out of the stream," I said to myself. "It is five times as large."

# 17

FOUND A FIRE burning in camp and three pairs of boots set out to dry, but the men had gone.

Now that I was alone I opened my hand and looked at the nugget. Before, when I had seen it at dawn, the color was subdued, but in the sun the whole thing glittered and shone. Carefully I wrapped it in a piece of cloth cut from my jerkin.

"It is bigger than a chestnut and pure gold," I said to myself. "It must weigh twenty *onzas*. Perhaps more!"

I laid the nugget away, at the bottom of the small pouch used for paints, and put it out of mind. I spread my materials on a stone, thinking to start on the map I had planned. But as I began to work my thoughts kept returning to the stream, to the gold I had seen and had not picked up. There might be other pieces lying on the sandy bottom as large as the one hidden in the pouch.

At last, because the work did not progress, I decided to make a small and simpler map, of the Abyss and the river and the location of Nexpan. The other could wait for a better time. But this one was also slow to take shape and

I was about to give up when Zia came out of the grove and threw herself down at my side.

"Chief Quantah and Father Francisco have talked since you left, never stopping," she said. "Each one spoke for himself, but I had to speak for both of them. First one and then the other. My tongue is dry like a stick."

Silent for only a moment, she sat up and asked what colors I would use for the map, what it was about, and could she help. Montezuma stared out at me from her pocket, twitching its sharp nose.

I did not tell her that I was getting ready to go down to the stream. "The map concerns the Abyss," I said. "The blue dots are the pines that grow high on the rampart."

"Where are the cottonwood trees?" she asked.

"Lower down. By the river. I have not come to them yet."

"When you come to them, will they be blue?"

"No, yellow. Because their leaves have begun to turn."

"For the river you will use blue."

"No, *amiga.*"

"But the river is blue."

Zia liked this color best of all. To her the most beautiful map in the world would be one where everything was blue.

"The river is green," I said.

She shook her head so hard that the bells on her hat sounded more like the buzz of a rattlesnake.

"If the cottonwood trees that are green you make yellow," she said, "and the blue river you make green, then the map will not be a true map of this country."

"It is not necessary," I said, "for a map to look like the country. It needs only to look like a map."

She turned her back upon me and raised her face toward the high, thin line of the ramparts, pale against th sky.

"The map you will make I do not wish to see. Nor do I wish to help with it." She was quiet a moment or two, thinking. "What I wish is that I could be there with Señor Torres."

"And the foal?"

"Yes, with the horse which is called Blue Star. And I would ride around on its back through the pine trees. And . . ."

"The river," I broke in, "will be ultramarine, just for you, which as I have said is the most glorious of blues. There is more. Do you remember the small island in the river which we passed? Well, to that island I will give a name."

She glanced at me. "What name?"

"I will call it La Isla de la Señorita."

"For me?"

"For you."

She bounded from the grass, laughing, and threw her arms around me and pressed her forehead against my cheek. Montezuma, caught between us, gave out a small squeak.

It was then that the three men came staggering into camp.

"More fire," Mendoza whispered through lips stiff with cold.

I stirred the fire and they clustered around it. In each of the helmets was a double handful of gold, but when I spoke about their good fortune no one answered. In the silence I heard the chattering of teeth.

At last Roa said, "I could fill a dozen helmets."

"And freeze unto death while you fill one," Zuñiga said.

"We shall fill a dozen," Mendoza said. "But hear me. We shall not freeze."

He left the fire and in a short time returned with his dirk and a small stone. He sat down, thrust his bare feet toward the blaze, and began to sharpen the knife.

"You risk our lives," I said, "if you kill Quantah's sheep."

"We die from cold if we do not," Mendoza answered.

"The Chief will remember how the tree was toppled," Roa said. "We can topple him also."

Mendoza said nothing more, but the knife slid back and forth across the stone. The honing ceased. I saw Father Francisco emerge from the grove, singing in his cracked voice. Mendoza hid the knife in his jerkin.

Father Francisco glanced at the gold. "You have reaped much," he said, "but I have reaped more. When the sun rises tomorrow it will shine on a new cross. We have built one from oak and it stands eight cubits high."

The little priest spread wide his arms to show us how the cross stood.

"It has a crooked shape as I have," he said, "yet it is a cross." He moved around in an awkward jig, the skirts of his gray robe flying. He did this always when he was struck with happiness. Abruptly the dance ended and he pointed to each of us in turn. "I will need your help with the mass. Also with the baptism. There are more than nine hundred souls."

Mendoza said, "Nine hundred. That requires a week. Our days here grow short. I will think of a quicker way to baptize than one at a time. I will make a mop of river rushes and with such a mop and a big gourd of water all may be sprinkled at once."

Father Francisco turned a fierce eye upon him.

Mendoza feigned surprise. "Surely you know of that. It is a very old method. Used when my grandfather was a young man in Granada, as I recall by a Bishop Cisneros. When the Moors were driven from the city, to save their lives and possessions they rushed to accept the Faith. So many infidels filled the churches that it was necessary to baptize them by mops twirled over their heads. If a bishop can employ a mop, so can you, dear Father."

Not waiting for an answer, Mendoza rose and motioned to Roa and Zuñiga. "We go now," he said, "to gather rushes for the mop."

I watched them disappear, knowing their true purpose, but powerless to hold them back.

Night fell and they did not return. We ate supper with Chief Quantah and again he asked why Mendoza was hungrier for gold than for food, to which Father Francisco gave the same reply as before. We went back to camp and built up the fire and sat talking. Still the three did not return.

I woke near midnight to the sound of footsteps. It was

134

the men coming up from the stream. They threw more wood on the fire and stood around it, talking in whispers. The firelight shone on their doublets. It was the shine of blood.

# 18

BEFORE DAWN the Indians of Nexpan gathered in front of their ancient altar and the tall, oak cross that had been newly made for them. Beside the cross stood Chief Quantah and Father Francisco, and behind the priest stood Zia and I. The three men were also there, though they had come late, in doublets carefully cleaned of blood. They had slept little that night and wished to sleep more, but feared Father Francisco's wrath.

While we waited for the sun to rise, Zuñiga whispered in my ear, "The fleece are anchored on the stream. Six of them. Thick ones which will collect much gold."

The sun rose and with it came the cry of wonder. Chief Quantah spoke the three words.

Waiting stiffly as the incantation was three times repeated, Father Francisco suffered the pagan ceremony because he must. But as it ended he made a gesture, a quick jab of his forefinger into the air, which he often used to drive away the devil.

After he had read a brief service, which Zia translated as best she could, he began baptism. With the rush mop that Mendoza had made he soaked up water from a gourd and swung the mop back and forth. Drops sparkled in the sun and fell on the upturned faces of the Indians who stood near. At first they shrank away, then laughed and drew closer. Again he swung the mop, but this time he flicked the water towards those who stood far in the back.

Above the whispering and laughter, I heard a shout and the running of feet. From the edge of the grove, a voice cried one clear word. I had never heard the word before, and yet do not know its meaning, but in the space of a breath it silenced the crowd.

Over the heads of the people, I made out the man who had uttered the cry. He was emerging from the grove and in his hand was a shepherd's crook, which he held aloft. He cried the word once more and pointed the crook towards the altar.

"*Sancta Trinidad,*" Roa said.

"*La Trinidad,*" Zuñiga said, "*y todos los otros.*"

Mendoza said something under his breath.

The crowd moved forward slowly, as a spent wave moves upon the shore. There was no sound. I heard nothing except my own heart beating.

The Indians came closer, until the first reached the altar. Chief Quantah held up his hand to stay them. But quickly Mendoza seized his matchlock and fired over their heads. On the edge of the grove branches came crashing to earth. At the sound everyone turned.

The next moments I do not remember well, so confused they were. I do recall that Mendoza forced Father Francisco down from the altar. With Roa and Zuñiga brandishing their long dirks, we then made our way around the crowd, skirted the grove where we could be ambushed, and thus reached our camp.

We might have gone safely through the throng, for not a stone had been cast, nor a word spoken. I do not know. The only thing I heard was a sound of distress, a lament of sorrow and loss. I heard it still while we stood around our fire, deciding what to do. It came softly through the trees on the morning wind.

The decision was made to break camp. At most we had only another two days to leave the Abyss. Before we started, Father Francisco said he was going back to talk with Quantah.

"I go to ask his forgiveness. Although I myself do not forgive this act."

Mendoza was sullen. "It is not a matter of forgiveness," he said. "The cacique owns a thousand sheep and more. We have killed six."

"If he owned ten times that number," Father Francisco said, "and did not wish one killed, it would be wrong to do so."

"You go at your own peril," Mendoza replied. "And I do not go with you. We are greatly outnumbered."

"I wish to go alone," said Father Francisco. "There is no danger."

Zia went and stood beside him, but telling her to stay he hobbled off by himself. As he disappeared into the grove, Mendoza gave orders to collect our things and to put all the gold in one helmet. The nugget, which was larger than a large chestnut, indeed thrice the weight of a stone of the same size, which lay wrapped in cloth at the bottom of my pouch, I left there, saying nothing.

"What happens to the fleece?" Roa asked.

"We take them," said Mendoza.

"But they have not yet had time to gather much gold."

"We take them anyway. If we delay, even until noon, it will give the Indians a chance to close the defile. Rocks rolled into the mouth would trap us here forever."

"I worry about that," Zuñiga said.

"I likewise," said Mendoza. "It is a matter of importance."

"I shall go and stir the sand," Roa said.

"Take Zuñiga," Mendoza said, "and when you are done drag the fleece out on the bank to dry."

The two men left for the stream and Zia and I began to put our few things in order. Mendoza paused to scan the meadow, the grove, the defile through which we would have to leave. The sound of lamenting could no longer be heard, possibly because the wind had changed and now blew in gusts from the north.

In a short time Father Francisco returned to say that the cacique had absolved us of wrongdoing. "Quantah offered food for our journey," he said. "It is waiting in the grove."

"We go without food," Mendoza answered. "I do not trust him nor his people." He pointed to a line of dark figures far off in the west, moving slowly toward the defile. "If you look carefully, esteemed Father, you will see some of them now. Can you assure me that Quantah has not sent them to bar our passage?"

"To me," Father Francisco said, "they are grazing deer."

I thought the same.

"It is your duty to save souls," Mendoza said. "It is mine to save lives. Our lives." He put on his helmet. "We go now and without the food. Pray that we reach the defile before it is closed."

As we set off, Mendoza hung back. When we came to the path that followed the stream, I turned to see where he was. He had not left the fire. He stood with his eyes fixed on the line of dark figures, moving at the base of the cliff.

Suddenly, while I watched, he seized a burning faggot and threw it into the dry grass. He threw another and ran. I looked for Father Francisco, wondering if he had seen, but he was hidden by a willow copse.

"That will give the Indians something to think about," Mendoza said, overtaking me. "Both those in the grove and those skulking along the cliff."

Small rings of flame surrounded the two faggots, as we stood watching, and I thought they would die out. Mendoza thought so too for he was on the point of going back to rekindle them when they were caught up by a gust of wind.

With a roar that seemed to shake the earth beneath my feet, the flames joined and in one vast sheet, which covered most of the surrounding meadow, leaped skyward. Actually, the fire had crept stealthily through the grass, unseen by us, until it was struck by the wind.

Hurrying on, we came to Roa and Zuñiga. They had

just driven a small flock of sheep across the stream, thus to stir the sand and float the gold flakes over the anchored fleece. They now stood on the near bank, watching the fire.

"Drag out the fleece," Mendoza shouted. "You can observe the fire afterwards."

It took time to do this, for the fleece were heavy with gold. From them we pressed the water as best we could, but even so we could carry only four, one to each of us.

Zia and Father Francisco, who were farther along the path, had stopped to watch the fire. Staggering along under our burdens, we overtook them.

Mendoza said, "The fire is a great misfortune, revered Father. I thought that it had died out. But the wind, the wind searched around in the ashes and found a spark."

Father Francisco looked at Mendoza, squinting his eyes. But so regretfully had the captain spoken, so humble were his words, that if any doubts crossed the priest's mind they were fleeting.

"The wind found a small spark, Father. A very small one. Now behold it!"

"I behold it." Father Francisco crossed himself. "What can be done?"

"Nothing," said Mendoza. "It will soon burn itself out. But let us go and quickly."

He gave the helmet, which was half-filled with gold, to me and we started off.

The fire had raced through the meadow, through a field of unharvested corn, and had nearly reached the south bastion. Sheep and deer and other animals that I

141

did not recognize fled before it. Three boys, whose task it was to guard the corn, were fleeing also.

We had traveled most of the distance to the defile when suddenly Zuñiga dropped his fleece and said that he would go back for another. Since he had the strength of two men, Mendoza permitted him to go.

In a short time we came to the defile and found to our relief that the entrance was open. Rocks piled on either side of it had not been moved. The dark figures, which earlier we had seen moving at the foot of the bastion, had disappeared.

Mendoza pointed to where, with a fleece over his back, Zuñiga ran along the path. I saw him stop to pick up the second fleece and move on.

"If he gets here," Mendoza said, laughing, "I will send him back for another."

Zuñiga had traveled more than halfway, to a bend in the stream, and to a second bend, when the wind lessened. Like an animal at bay, the flames moved in one direction, then another. Slowly the wind shifted, gained strength and blew hard from the south.

Zuñiga was not yet within hearing, but Francisco shouted for him to drop the fleece. "Run, *hombre*. Run for your life," he cried.

Fed by the wind and the bone-dry grass, the flames twisted, veered sidewise and in a wide curve swept down upon the stream.

Perhaps Zuñiga failed to see that the wind had changed. Perhaps he thought to outrun the fire. Whichever it was, he did not drop the fleece. He came on, stumbled under the heavy load, picked himself up, again slung it on his back, and started toward us.

Francisco, knowing he did not mean to leave the fleece behind, once more shouted a warning. Zuñiga looked up. I could see his face clearly. Then a wall of flame roared over him and he was lost to view.

The flames forced us back into the mouth of the defile. The four of us stood there in the darkness and looked out at the blazing fields. There was no sign anywhere of Zuñiga and the fleece.

*The Fortress of San Juan de Ulúa*
*Vera Cruz, in New Spain*
*The seventh day of October*
*The year of our Lord's birth, 1541*

THE COURTROOM, on the third day of my trial, is the same as before. The three old judges sit at the long, oak table, dressed in black, fur-trimmed robes, more like *zopilotes* than ever. The clerks sit primly in their places. Counsel Gamboa and the royal fiscal talk together. Don Felipe stands behind me, shuffling his feet.

The courtroom is the same, except that in the part held for spectators there are more of them than before. Judging from their clothes, the newcomers are from Vera Cruz. My fame has spread, or rather the news of the treasure that lies hidden in the Land of Cíbola.

After I have taken the oath, the royal fiscal says pleasantly, as if we were acquaintances meeting in the plaza, "Do you find prison fare to your liking? Is it cooked well? Is it plentiful?"

"Often I have eaten worse and also less," I answer.

"And the bed?"

"Many nights I have slept on the ground."

"Then you like our prison? It is a place where you could spend many happy hours?"

I do not answer. The fiscal takes a sheaf of papers from

144

the table, which he studies while pulling at his lower lip. He puts the papers down and looks at me.

I expect him to begin where he left off on the first day of the trial. But he takes a different tack and asks me to tell the Audiencia in my own words (whose words would I use if I did not use my own?), about the battle of Háwikuh.

"What was your part in that battle?" he directs me.

I start at the beginning, at the place when I followed Captain Mendoza into the city. I describe how we reached the first terrace and how the Indians hurled rocks upon us.

I have the feeling, as these things are recounted, that the fiscal has heard them before, from someone else. I tell of the attack by the young Indian and the struggle that followed and how we both lay wounded on the terrace.

Here the fiscal interrupts me. "How bad were the wounds you suffered?"

"Bad, sir."

"Will you describe them?"

I do so.

"The wound on your head. Was it the worst?"

"Yes, sir."

"How long did it take you to recover from this wound?"

"Several weeks. Three."

"Not longer?"

"No, sir."

"You have recovered from this wound?"

"As far as I know."

The royal fiscal glances at the judges. "As far as you

know," he says, "you have recovered. But you are not certain."

Aware of my mistake, I say, "I am certain."

"One moment you are not certain. The next moment you are."

"I am certain."

"But is it not true that for a month after you left Háwikuh you were troubled by pains in your head and by poor vision?"

"I did have trouble."

"The trouble is gone?"

"Yes, sir."

Again the fiscal looks at his papers. "When you left Háwikuh," he asks, "how much gold did you carry?"

"None, sir, because none was found there."

"The first gold. Where did you find it?"

"In the City of Nexpan."

"Will you tell the Audiencia how it was found and in what amounts?"

In detail I recount the story of the stream and of the fleece, of the fire and how Zuñiga was consumed in it. Once more I feel that, like that of Háwikuh, he knows this story. Who could have told him? Who surely but Torres, the armorer, the blacksmith, the thief?

"This was the first gold," the fiscal says. "What did it weigh?"

"It filled one helmet by half. And there were three fleece."

"Enough, then, for you to quarrel over," the royal fiscal says.

146

"There was no quarrel," I reply.

"None?"

Before I can answer Counsel Gamboa is on his feet, trying to talk for one reason or another. Meanwhile, the fiscal glances through his sheaf of papers.

I notice for the first time that on the outside of the sheaf he holds is a red seal. These are not his own papers, therefore, but papers sent to him from somewhere, possibly by the Viceroy or from the frontier in Guadalajara. And in them is the testimony of a sworn witness. The testimony of Guillermo Torres? Yes, of Guillermo Torres, the thief.

My counsel is told politely by one of the judges to sit down, which he does.

"About this matter of the quarrel," the fiscal says, "after you found the gold . . . ?"

"There was no quarrel," I repeat.

"About anything?"

"Well, one between Captain Mendoza and Father Francisco."

The fiscal glances at the ceiling in despair. "First there is no quarrel. Then there is a quarrel. Remember, Señor Sandoval, that you speak under the oath of the cross. Tell me what the quarrel was about."

"About the fire. The cause of the fire. And the death of Zuñiga."

"During these quarrels . . ."

"There was only one," I break in.

"During these quarrels," the fiscal continues, "which side were you on?"

"On neither side."

The fiscal turns and speaks to the judges.

"Your Excellencies, we have a fire which caused the death of one Baltasar Zuñiga. The priest, Father Francisco, accuses Captain Mendoza of starting the fire. Captain Mendoza, denying the accusation, says that it was caused by an accident. The young man who stands before you was present at this quarrel. And yet he claims that he favored neither one side nor the other."

The fiscal faces me. "You had no opinion in this matter?" he asks.

"I had an opinion."

"But you did not express it. Why?"

"Because Mendoza was our captain."

The fiscal smiles. "In other words, you were really against Captain Mendoza in this quarrel. You thought him guilty."

I see my error, but it is too late.

The fiscal goes on, "And because in your mind he was guilty, you actually threatened his life. What did Captain Mendoza say when you made this threat?"

"I made no threat." The trick of putting words in my mouth I am now familiar with. "None, sir."

"Let us see," the fiscal says. "You were recovering from a severe wound at this time. You were, in fact, suffering from pains and poor vision. Is it true?"

"Yes, sir."

"Then it is possible, is it not, that what you did at this time is really not clear to you now? That you have forgotten what took place?"

"There are things I do not remember, but I remember this."

"You remember that you did threaten Captain Mendoza?"

"No, sir."

"You have forgotten that you threatened Captain Mendoza?"

"No sir. I mean . . ."

The royal fiscal strolls to the window and looks out at the sea. It is silvery and calm, the color of hot lead. I am confused by all his questions. Since I have pleaded guilty to the charge of defrauding the King, why does he ask them?

He leaves the window and crosses the room towards me. He has an odd way of walking. He puts his toes down first, then his heels, and then as his heels strike the floor, he bounces up on them, with a little jerk. It is the walk of a man well satisfied with himself.

He stops within a pace of me and says in a soft voice, almost as if he were talking to himself, "I shall prove to the Royal Audiencia that the threat against Captain Mendoza's life, which we have discussed, is only the first of many such threats."

He glances at the onlookers in the back of the courtroom. They have been restless throughout the questioning, disappointed, I believe, that little has been said about the treasure.

"I shall prove," he says, raising his voice, "that the accused made many threats against the life of Captain Mendoza."

A suspicion crosses my mind. Since the questions I have answered had nothing to do with my crime against the King, they were asked for a different reason. Something that Guillermo Torres has accused me of and which I know nothing about.

"I shall prove," the fiscal says, "that these threats, repeated over a period of time, in the end led to a fight. And that this fight resulted in the death of Captain Blas de Mendoza at the hands of the accused, Estéban de Sandoval."

The courtroom is silent. I hear Don Felipe whispering over and over, *"Madre de Dios,"* like an old crone, and the onlookers muttering among themselves and Counsel Gamboa on his feet with a shout and one of the judges rapping on the table.

The royal fiscal walks away with his self-satisfied step. I watch him while he stops at the table to drink a cup of water, while he thumbs through the sheaf of papers which are stamped with the official seal, which hold the testimony of Guillermo Torres. Torres, who once was a thief and now is a liar. I am calm, if memory serves me, much calmer than at this moment as I sit here at my bench.

After Counsel Gamboa has spoken, one of the judges announces the end of the session. The trial will begin again in three days, on the tenth day of October.

"What a misfortune," Don Felipe says, while we are walking back to my cell. "And just when things were going well for us, or as well as could be hoped for."

I say nothing in reply. It is another hot day, with waves of heat rising above the leaden sea, but chills run down my back, thinking of the charge that has now been brought against me.

Before Don Felipe can ask about Mendoza's death, we have reached the cell, and there Counsel Gamboa is waiting. Gamboa insists upon speaking to me alone, so Don Felipe is forced to leave. This displeases him because he thinks of me, or so he says, as a son, and therefore should be privy to all that I do.

Gamboa waits until the jailer's steps fade in the passage. "The Royal Audiencia," he says, "will bring the charge the fiscal has requested. May I ask, before we go further . . . did you murder Blas de Mendoza?"

His question has an ominous sound, even here in my cell.

"I am innocent."

Judging from his expression, Counsel Gamboa does not believe me. "It is best to tell me the truth," he says.

"This is the truth," I answer, and not too patiently, I fear.

"As I thought," he says to calm me down. "But I wish to be certain. The royal fiscal will call a witness in an attempt to prove the charge of murder. His name is Guillermo Torres. At this moment, I have learned, he is in Vera Cruz."

Gamboa watches me closely, waiting, I suspect, for me to change my mind at this news and admit my guilt. I am silent.

"Who is this man?" he asks. "Since you are innocent of the charge, what is his purpose in coming here to testify against you?"

Torres, it is. I am surprised and not surprised. Anger tightens my throat, yet I manage to tell Gamboa all that I know about him from the time we met on the ship until I saw him last in the winter of '40.

"Why he wishes to accuse me of murder, I do not understand."

"Did you have the gold when you saw him last?"

"Only what would fill two helmets."

"The sixty thousand *onzas* were found later?"

"Months later. The next spring."

"Could Torres have heard of the treasure?"

"They have heard of it in the City of Mexico. On the frontier, in Guadalajara and other places."

"Then we can assume that he knows about it," my counsel says. "Do you suppose that he would testify against you if he thought that by so doing he would receive a share of the treasure? Is he capable of such an act."

"Torres," I answer, "is capable of any act."

My counsel gets up from the bench and straightens the frayed cuffs of his doublet. "Sixty thousand *onzas* of gold," he says. "One could do much with that amount. I have a father, who is crippled and cannot work, and three sisters and three young brothers to support. If I had two handfuls of the treasure, it would . . ." He pauses, looks at his frayed cuffs, and takes his leave.

I have more faith in him than before, yet I still have

doubts, mostly about his youth. It is one thing for him to defend me on the charge of defrauding the King, especially since I have plead guilty to this crime. It is something else for him to defend me against the charge of murder, facing a man as cunning and experienced as the royal fiscal. It is as if I were to compete in the subject of cartography with Mercator or Amerigo Vespucci.

My supper is fulsome, made up as it is of delicacies from the officers' table. Though I have no hunger, I make a show of eating to please Don Felipe, who hovers over me as if it is to be my last meal.

A wind has sprung up. The sky is cast over with rain clouds, which hide the star I have seen each evening. It is difficult for me to put the trial out of my thoughts, but I shall try. Before I again face the Royal Audiencia, it is necessary to write of those events that took place in the winter of '40 and the spring of '41, so they will be fresh in my mind once more.

# 19

THE SUN SHONE HOT in a clear sky as we started our climb out of the Abyss. But when we reached the rim, where Torres waited with the animals, the air was gray and heavy and smelled of snow.

Although our hoard of gold now filled two helmets brimming full, Mendoza decided not to return to Háwikuh.

"I think that Chief Quantah spoke the truth," he said, "about the stream that has much gold and flows into the stream at Nexpan. But I do not recall how far it is."

"He did not say," I answered.

"It is called Tawhi," Roa broke in.

"We know that," Mendoza said.

"The Cloud City," Roa continued. "It is a journey of eight suns into the northwest."

"How is it that you know so much," Mendoza asked, "when I know nothing?"

"I talked to one of the Indians."

Mendoza glanced at Zia, who nodded her head, agreeing with Roa.

"The Cloud City is eight suns away," she said.

Without further talk, the *conducta* set off, moving fast for we feared a storm.

We traveled all day, under cloudy skies, until we could see no longer. That night, powdery snow began to drift down through the pines. At dawn it was ankle-deep and still falling. But the horses were fresh, the Abyss lay behind us, our way trended into lower country, so we had good hopes of outriding the storm.

We would have escaped had the blue roan not lost a shoe.

Mendoza discovered the loss a little after midday. Because iron shoes were of great value, being scarce, and the snow had ceased, we retraced the trail to where the roan had stumbled over a hidden rock. The shoe was not found, and we lost two hours. By this margin the storm caught us.

Snow began to fall again late in the afternoon, softly at first, then in wind-driven flurries. Between flurries we caught glimpses of an open mesa about two leagues away and below us, where the sun was shining. We spurred our horses into a *pasotrote*.

Near this time, while crossing a meadow and a small stream fringed by willows, Zia pointed out a cave high on the face of a cliff. On the way from Háwikuh we had explored several of such caves and had found pieces of turquoise and silver, besides fine earthen pots which were of no use to us. But it was now a race against the storm and we did not tarry.

We had gone no farther than three hundred *varas* before the wind burst out of the north. Soon the air was

155

thick with snow, blinding both rider and horse, so thick that I, at the rear of the *conducta,* could not see our captain who rode in the lead.

Shouting, Mendoza pulled aside under a pine tree and waited for us to catch up.

"We cannot go on," he said, "though an hour's ride will bring us to the open mesa. Nor remain long where we are. We shall return to seek shelter in the cave which we have passed."

He himself took the halter of the mule that carried the gold.

"And hear me," he said. "Do not straggle. Keep together. Be quick. A more monstrous storm I have not beheld since the days of the Sierra Nevadas."

The trail we had just made was now covered by drifts, yet we safely reached the meadow, and by following the stream, the cliff. At its base was an overhang of rock, which formed a long gallery, large enough to protect the animals. By a series of handholds cut into the cliff, we clambered aloft to the lower lip of the cave.

Snow lay there, but within, the cave was dry, possibly thirty paces in depth and width, twice the height of a tall man. In one corner was a pile of half-burned logs, sifted over with dust which might have been the dust of centuries, and beside it a pile of faggots. Ranged neatly against the wall nearby was a row of earthen pots.

The cave was similar to those we had already seen, even to the wood and utensils. It was as if, long ago, those who had lived here had suddenly left, from hunger or fear of enemies. The bones we found, as in the other caves, belonged not to humans but to deer and coyote.

We made ourselves at home, first by building a fire. Our store of dried meat was enough to last five or six days, so we cooked a good meal and ate with relish, making lame jokes about the snow, lame because we were still very cold and far from the city of Tawhi.

"What did the Indians tell you about this Cloud City?" Mendoza asked Zia.

"All that they told me, Roa told you," Zia answered.

"It is nothing," Mendoza said.

"Yes, nothing," Zia said.

Below us the horses were restless and she went to the lip of the cave and listened. She was more concerned about the foal than about the Cloud City.

"Since it is nothing," Mendoza said, "we shall not be disappointed with what we find there."

"We shall find Indians," said Father Francisco, who as usual was more interested in souls to save than in treasure. "As we did at Nexpan."

Torres said, "If it is a journey of seven days to your Cloud City, it likewise will be seven days returning. On top of that, to reach Háwikuh, means eleven days more. In all, twenty-five days. Over two hundred leagues of hard travel. Horseshoes are scarce. Do we have sufficient to last for such a long journey?"

"Sufficient," Mendoza answered, closing the subject.

Our most serious problem was feed for the animals. Torres had gathered bundles of dry grass while he waited for us at the Abyss, and these they now were eating. But on the morrow more feed must be found.

Snow fell through the night and when we climbed down from the cave it lay waist-deep in the meadow. Working together, we cut willow branches along the stream, ample feed for that day and the next.

About noon, with a wan sun at the top of the cliff, Captain Mendoza saddled the roan and struck off through the meadow, saying that he would try to make a trail which we could follow.

Fearfully, I watched him go, the horse rearing high on her back legs as she came to the first drift, then settling down to rear again. Thus I saw them disappear.

"A fool's errand," Torres said, and some agreed.

We waited beside the fire through the afternoon, but near nightfall, when it began to snow again, Roa got up and said that he was going in search of the captain. While he was saddling his horse, Mendoza appeared, so stiff from cold he needed to be helped down from the roan.

"I traveled no farther than we did yesterday," he said. "We will have to wait for a thaw or until the snow hardens, if it takes a month."

That night we ate another good meal and made more jokes about the storm. Next day, in need of wood, we spent many hours cutting dead branches, which we pulled up to the cave by means of picket ropes tied together. That night, as I remember, we ate less, but there was still food enough for three or four days and we were not worried.

"If we have to," Torres said, "we can kill one of the mules. There is enough meat on a mule to last for weeks."

"Excellent meat, too," said Roa. "It requires the teeth of a shark, yet gives strength and is the equal of any."

"To those who are hungry," Torres said. "But I have also eaten the hide. That was on the *entrada* into Yucatán with General Vejar."

"How is the taste of a mule hide? I have often wondered about this," Roa asked.

"If the weather does not change," Mendoza said, "you will soon know."

"Tough, I am certain," said Roa.

"That depends upon several factors," Torres said. "The hide must be from a young mule. Nothing ancient. But of chief importance is the preparation. You first cut the hide into pieces of the right size to fit the pot. These you singe over a hot fire, removing all hair. Then they are scraped clean and put into the pot to boil. The boiling takes many hours and should not be hurried by an impatient eye. Not until the pieces are very soft and melt together in one mass do you cease the boiling. Then you set the pot aside and allow the mass to cool. When it is cold and stiff, you have a jelly, which is gray in color and looks like glue."

"How is the taste?" Roa asked again.

"Like glue," said Torres. "Loathsome."

"With pepper and salt?"

"Equally."

"But strength-giving?"

"Yes," said Torres, "it gives much strength."

Mendoza fingered his beard. "We shall eat no mules,

young nor old," he said, thinking perhaps of treasure and the mules needed to transport it. "First, before that comes to pass, we shall eat one another."

"This I have also seen," said Torres. "In the summer of '29. On the great desert of Vizcaíno."

While Torres told about his ill-fated journey, a south wind began to blow and by morning the sky was clear and water ran everywhere. That day we cut willow for the animals and made ready to leave the next dawn.

# 20

HE WIND died during the night, but the sound of water went on, trickles of it from the roof of the cave, a roar from the stream in the meadow. It was like a thaw in springtime.

I awakened near daylight to the stamping of horses. A moment or two later I thought that I heard someone call my name. The voice came from far off, or seemed to, not from the cave. I sat up and listened, straining my ears, but heard nothing more, except the loud running of water.

Around me my companions were asleep, all save Guillermo Torres. It was his voice, then, that I had heard, calling from below. Deliberately, I pulled on my boots, pausing several times to listen. One of my chores was to help him curry the horses, which I was never happy to do, and no more on this morning than others.

I found my doublet, which I shook free of dust and carefully straightened. As I slipped it on, I glanced beyond the fire at Zia's pallet of pine needles set against the wall. I always rose before she did and, as on this morning, my eyes never failed to seek her out. The habit of sleeping on her back, with both hands clasped beneath her head, amused me. I was amused too, and touched, by her face when she was asleep. It had the look of a very small child, so different from the serious, grown-up face she wore at other times.

I glanced twice in her direction, and walked around the fire to look again before I realized that the pallet was empty. She was nowhere around. She had left the cave. Seized by sudden fear, remembering the voice that had called to me, I hurried outside and gazed down into the meadow.

At the entrance to the cavern the snow was trampled as if animals had been milling about. I saw that hoof tracks led away from the cavern, followed the stream across the meadow and disappeared in a clump of dwarf pines. The tracks were faint in the mushy snow. How many horses or mules had made them, I could not tell. But it was plain to me that they led in the direction of the Abyss, toward Háwikuh.

I shouted an alarm to those who were asleep beside the fire and began my precarious descent of the cliff. Water had frozen in the handholds during the night so my progress was slow, one thin hold at a time. Near the bottom I lost my grip and slid heavily to earth. There for a while I lay, half-stunned.

I became aware of sounds, of stealthy movements, close by, within the cavern.

Still dazed, my face buried in the snow, I lifted my head and wiped the snow away. The sounds had ceased. Then from above me came a shout and I looked up to see Roa crouched at the lip of the cave. I pointed to the tracks that led off across the meadow.

Slowly I got to my feet. As my head cleared and I heard distinctly the ring of spurs, Torres rode out of the cavern.

He sat astride the blue roan. The foal was at her heels. Tied to the hind bow of his saddle were the two sacks which held the gold gathered at Nexpan.

I do not know if he had heard me fall from the cliff, but he heard me as I shouted and ran toward him. When I was about five paces away, he grasped at the rondel dagger which he carried in a sheath fastened to his thigh.

There was a drift of snow in front of him and he had to cross it and the stream to reach the meadow. I think that he must have seen Roa, at the base of the cliff, unsling his matchlock, for instead of drawing the dagger, he hesitated.

I was behind Torres now, so close I could touch his horse. My hope was to seize the bridle and thus stop him for a moment, long enough for Roa to use the matchlock.

In the midst of this — of Roa's taking aim, of Torres' reaching for his dagger, then changing his mind, of my trying to grasp the bridle, and then, from the lip of the cave, Mendoza firing a shot which missed its mark — in the moment or two that all this took place, a thought went through my mind. Zia and Torres are in a plot together, against us. Zia has taken the other horses and left. Fleeing the camp, it is she who has left tracks in the snow.

The thought was still in my mind, and a feeling of shock at her treachery, when suddenly Zia came out from

163

the cavern. She had been injured by a blow, for there was a gash on her forehead and blood ran down one cheek.

"Drop, *hombre!*" Roa shouted behind me.

I knew that I was in his way, but I was thinking of Zia and did not heed the command.

Torres, at Roa's outcry, spurred his horse and with one lunge was through the drift and into the stream.

Five or six steps behind the roan, as Torres set the spurs, the foal leaped ahead to catch up.

"Hold her," Zia cried to me, as Blue Star went by. "Hold her!"

I tried but the foal swerved and by a small margin eluded my grasp. Zia was beside me now. As the foal reached the drift it paused. Zia threw herself desperately forward and caught one leg.

"*Por Dios!*" she cried, as the two of them went down in a flurry of snow. "Help," she sobbed, and with all her strength clung to the struggling foal.

Before I could move, the foal broke Zia's hold. It rose, stumbled, and ran straight into my arms. Together we crashed to earth.

Meanwhile, so I was told, for I was too busy to know, Torres had spurred his horse through the stream. As they reached the far bank the roan had heard the neigh of her foal and swung about. But under heavy bit and rowel Torres turned her head and forced her into a gallop. The shots fired by Roa went wide. By the time Mendoza reloaded his matchlock, Torres was disappearing in the trees.

My struggle with the foal ended quickly when Roa tied

her legs with a rope. We left her with Zia and ran to the cavern. Mendoza was already there, saddling a horse and shouting threats against Torres.

"You will never overtake him," Roa said. "Remember, he rides the roan."

"I remember," said Mendoza. "Also that he carries the gold. I remember both. Give me your dagger, Roa. Mine I left in the cave."

Mendoza had chosen the best of the horses that were left, a big sorrel, which was no match for the roan, either over a short distance or long. Yet, so great was his rage, I wondered if he might not overtake Torres by force of will. He was capable of pursuing him for days or weeks, for whatever time was needed.

Mendoza threw a saddle on the gray's back and reached for the girth, then drew back in surprise.

"Cut," he said, quietly. "Cut in two." He turned and, running to where the other three saddles lay, examined the girths. "Each one. All of them, the same," he said.

"It is well," said Roa. "Otherwise, who knows where the night would find you? Or us? Already the clouds gather and the wind blows."

We stood looking at the tracks leading off through the meadow, in the direction of Háwikuh, at the lowering sky. Then Roa made a halter for the foal and tethered it to a tree.

Mendoza spoke to Zia. She had washed the blood from her face in the snow, but she was still pale.

"What took place?"

"Much took place," Zia said.

"Tell us."

"I tell what I can," Zia said slowly through lips that were tight with pain.

"Later, perhaps," Mendoza said. "When you talk better."

"Now," Zia said, "when I have my hat, which is in the cavern."

I went for the hat and, brushing her hair back, she put it on.

"I was sleeping," she said, "but I heard Blue Star neigh. It is a dream, I thought. Again I heard this sound. Then I thought it is not a dream and I ran outside the cave and looked down in the meadow. Light was coming through the forest and I saw Señor Torres ride across the stream. He had been out and was coming back, for I saw tracks in the snow where he had gone out. He rode into the cavern and Blue Star neighed again. There was a sound. It was the sound when you break a branch from a tree. Blue Star went outside the cave and stood there. I thought, yes, the sound was when Señor Torres struck her and he will do this again. So I climbed down the cliff."

"You did not think of the gold?" Mendoza said.

"No, I thought of Blue Star."

"You did not call?"

"No. Next time I will call."

"You climbed down," Mendoza said. "Then . . ."

"Then I went to the cavern quickly. Señor Torres had a dagger and he sat on a saddle cutting something. He did not see me. The horse, which belongs to the Captain, stood near and I saw the two sacks of gold on its back. And when I did, Señor Torres turned his head to listen. But he saw me and jumped and caught my arm. I screamed and he hit me. I do not remember more to tell."

"There is not much more," Mendoza said. "Except that I am a poor shot with the matchlock and Roa is worse and Sandoval is *nada*. And we have four girths to mend before we leave. Of the gold, we shall say nothing. Nor of that sweepings of the world's stables, Guillermo Torres."

He paused and glanced about him. Finally, his eyes rested on the big dog, who sat watching us from the shelter of a bush.

"Tigre!" he shouted and, as the dog trotted over, wagging his tail, gave him a slap across the ears. "You are a lout, Tigre. And your former master was a lout. I know now why he wished to sell you. It was for the reason that you should belong to some old lady." He gave the big dog another slap on the head, and glanced at Roa. "You did not teach him much."

"He is not a good student," said Roa.

Father Francisco, who like Tigre had slept through most of the adventure and had only appeared while Zia was talking, now read the morning service. We rose from our knees in better spirits and began to mend the slashed saddle girths, which was no small task.

Before noon we were on the way to Tawhi, the City of Clouds, unaware that we would not see it until the winter had gone and another spring had come.

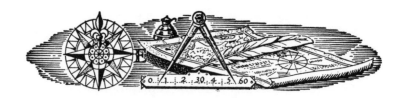

*The Fortress of San Juan de Ulúa*
*Vera Cruz, in New Spain*
*The eighth day of October*
*The year of our Lord's birth, 1541*

THE WALLS OF San Juan de Ulúa are made of coral stone, hewn into blocks and carefully fitted together. At the top, my jailer tells me, they are six *varas* in thickness, six full steps across. At the bottom, where the walls rest upon the rocky bed of the sea, they are nine *varas*. The fortress itself is so vast that it would take a man the better part of an hour to walk its circumference.

So vast, indeed, that once, standing on the balcony of his palace in Spain, the King shaded his eyes and peered intently toward the west.

"For what is Your Majesty looking?" asked a courtier.

"For San Juan de Ulúa."

"That is thousands of leagues away, Your Majesty."

"Yes," replied Charles V, "but it has cost me enough to be seen across the sea."

Yet vast as it is, I swear that for a night and a day this stone fortress, which is larger than the great cathedral of Seville, which is larger than any fortress of the Christian world, has seemed to move like a ship at sea.

The wind began yesterday at dusk, with wisps of damp air curling through the window. By midnight it blows with such force that I have to leave my pallet and seek shelter in a corner of the cell, though the window is very small and barred by wide, iron bands.

There is no way to make the candle burn, so I crouch in the corner like a rat in a hole, and cannot write.

It is noon before I hear Don Felipe's steps in the passageway. The door, driven by the wind, crashes open and strains against its hinges. He tries to close it but fails. We both put our shoulders to the door, which strikes me as curious, indeed — a prisoner helping to imprison himself.

"For two hours I have been on the way," he says, setting my breakfast on the bench.

Usually, he is neat in polished jackboots and well-brushed doublet, but this morning he has the appearance of one who has just crawled forth from a chimney hole.

"What a wind!" he says. "A man cannot stand against it. So I came roundabout, a secret way, through passages I have not used in a year. This, *compañero,* accounts for my lateness and the coldness of the food."

Despite his appearance, he has a bright air about him. He is the bearer, I fear, of bad news.

I have no hunger, yet eat as I have before, to please him. He says nothing of importance until I am finished. He then takes from his inner doublet a roll of papers tied with leather thongs, which at once I recognize.

"Your notes," he says, handing them to me with a flourish. "All the way from the City of Mexico, safe and sound, though the messenger twice was accosted by bandits, once came near to losing his life in a flooding river,

169

and arrived just before the storm!"

I remove the stones from the hiding place in the floor, secrete the notes, and replace the stones.

"When do you begin the map?" Don Felipe says.

"When the wind dies."

"Do you make a large map?"

"As large as paper permits."

"With the trail that leads to Cíbola? Latitude? Mountains and rivers? Everything put down, *señor*, so that the treasure can be located without trouble?"

"Complete," I answer.

"How long does the map require?"

"Two days."

"Not sooner?"

"No."

Don Felipe looks at me and his eyes grow small. "What happens when you give the notes to the Royal Audiencia?"

"I keep a copy."

"Exact?"

"Exact."

"And by looking at the notes, just looking at them, the Audiencia can tell nothing?"

"Nothing."

"If they ask you to read the notes, to explain them, what do you say?"

"I say nothing."

"No, *señor*, this is what you say. You say, 'Sirs, these are the observations I made at the time I hid the treasure. There is nothing more, Your Excellencies, which I can add to them.' Do you understand? If you do, be so kind as to repeat all that I have just said."

I repeat it, word for word, and add a phrase or two of my own.

"Excellent," he says.

When he is gone (again I help him to close the door) I dig out the notes and, crouching in the corner, examine them. They have been stained in many places, likely at the time the messenger was caught by the flood. Still they can be read.

I look at them carefully — comments, figures, the two small sketches. They are more complete than I remember them. Yet they are misleading, even to a good cartographer.

Water is coming through the window from rain and the heavy seas. I decide to put the notes in my own hiding place in the wall, lest they be further damaged. It occurs to me that if the seas increase the whole cell will be flooded, but there is nothing I can do.

Shortly after my jailer leaves, I am visited by the commander of the fortress, Captain Martín. He has been blown about by the storm, though, like Don Felipe, he has apparently come by a secret passage.

"I shall deem it an honor," he says, "to go before the Royal Audiencia and testify in your behalf. To your good character. To the fact that I have known you on the frontier and think you incapable of murdering Mendoza. Though I must say, judging from what I have seen of him, that the temptation might have been great."

Captain Martín stays for more than an hour. We talk

about the summer in Háwikuh and the grand *jornado* he later made into the east. Not once does he mention the treasure, nor even hint at it. I enjoy his visit, as much as the first, and tell him so. The captain, I feel, is a friend, the only friend I have in the fortress of San Juan.

Now that night is here the wind has diminished, though seas still crash against the fortress walls. Waves rise nearly to the height of the window.

The sky is covered with thin, scaly clouds, so I cannot find the western star, whose name I should know.

It is two days before the trial starts again, scarcely time to write the story of our winter on the mesa, and that of Tawhi, as well. Since the sun shone there on the mesa, which was a day's journey from the cave, and food was plentiful, since one day was much like another, with Zia and me busy on our maps, Roa off hunting, Mendoza training his big dog, Tigre, and Father converting to the true faith the Indians who wandered by, and all of us at times making deerskin bags to carry the gold which Mendoza thought we would find, there is no need to do this.

It is better to begin when spring came and the snow melted on the mountains, when, traveling into the northwest, we came within sight of Tawhi, for then much happened to us that will never happen again.

# 21

ON THE TWELFTH DAY of April we reached the Cloud City.

Late in the afternoon of that day we forded a stream where snow-water ran swift between greening banks. We followed the stream across a pretty meadow and through a canyon and toward evening came out into open country. The sun was down but the light was still good. There before us, less than a league away, jutting up from the plain, we saw a small mountain.

The base of the mountain was covered with patches of pine and aspen, but halfway up the trees ended in purple cliffs. The cliffs were curiously shaped and as I looked at them against the pale sky they seemed to form the outlines of a ship. A ship afloat on a purple sea, moving into the west under full sail.

The light faded, the purple cliffs grew black, the ship disappeared from view. Then as we made camp I saw close above the mountain, resting upon it like a coronet, what I took to be faint clusters of stars.

They were instead the fires of Tawhi, for at dawn as the sun rose and shone on the mountain top, we saw before us the glittering walls of a city. The glitter, we knew from our experience at Háwikuh, was caused by mica and not by gold. Yet there was much excitement among us.

Before the sun was an hour high, we reached the wooded slopes and a well-worn trail which led through the forest to the base of a cliff. Here the trail climbed abruptly over stony slides, too rugged for our animals. Leaving them with Roa, the rest of us set off on foot, taking food for two days and all that remained of the trinkets.

Now as we climbed, the walls of the city were clearly in view. The sound of voices drifted down to us, and the fragrance of burning piñon.

The trail grew steeper until at last it came to an end upon a wide ledge. Directly above, at the height of eight or nine *varas*, we made out a gap in the walls. It was seemingly an entrance to the city, but between us and the entrance rose a sheer stone barrier, without crevice or handhold.

Mendoza shouted a greeting, using an Indian phrase which Zia gave him. He would have fired his matchlock had we not run low on powder, for this never failed to catch attention.

At once, two men appeared at the top of the barrier. They made gestures of friendship and then let down a ladder of woven reeds and creepers, which swayed perilously from side to side as we crept aloft.

Seen from the plain, the city looked huddled and small, not so striking to the eye, except for its location, as Háwikuh. But once we were through the entrance and had come to the end of a crooked byway, we stopped in amazement.

We stood facing a spacious plaza, more than two furlongs in circumference. It was roughly oval in shape, of earth packed hard and smooth, and dark red in color as if mixed with blood, as is our custom in Spain. At the western end, on the very edge of the cliff, was a mass of mud houses one and two stories in height. In the center of the plaza a spring gushed forth from mossy rocks.

The most amazing aspect of the city, however, lay to the east. Facing the sun when it rose was a small lake of deep, blue water, on which birds of many colors were floating. A path bordered with piñon trees circled the lake and added further to the parklike appearance.

We were soon surrounded by Indians, their black eyes darting here and there, taking in everything about us.

And what a strange sight we must have been to these people who had never seen a white man before. Father Francisco with his tonsored hair and long, gray robe, a wooden cross slung upon his back. Mendoza and I dressed in glittering cuirass and gilded helmets. Even Zia, though an Indian herself, must have astounded them with her leather jacket and skirt and the corncake hat hung with silver bells.

At last from among the throng a man, who had the bearing of a cacique, stepped forth and gave a lengthy speech of welcome. To which Captain Mendoza, through Zia, replied with his oft-repeated greetings and pronouncements.

The cacique, whose name was Tlascingo, or so it

sounded, wished to know about our great king and about our travels, whence we came and whence we were going.

Then he said, "Below, near to the forest, there is another man whose skin is white. With him are twelve animals, which look like the deer, but are much larger. Tell me about these animals. Are they good to roast over a fire and eat?"

"Their flesh is tough like these," Mendoza said with a straight face, pointing to his boots. "And what is worse, they poison the stomach."

"Why then do you have these animals?" the cacique asked.

"We have them to carry burdens and to ride upon."

The cacique did not understand, so Mendoza straddled his matchlock and galloped around in a circle.

Tlascingo nodded his head but did not smile. "Are these animals wild like the deer?" he said.

"Wilder than deer. Wilder than antelope. Wilder than the wolf coyote."

"What is it that this animal eats?"

"It eats many things. But like you and me it prefers meat, either fresh or roasted."

"Meat of the deer?"

"Of the deer. Also of the rabbit and the antelope. But better than all else it likes the flesh of humans."

The cacique was silent awhile, thinking this over. We always lived in fear that our animals would be stolen. To the Indians who asked about them, therefore, Zia or Mendoza told this same lie. And always it had served us well.

"These animals are very strange," the cacique said.

176

"Strange," said Mendoza. "And of very strange habits."

"Where does this animal find humans to eat?"

"He finds them only when we kill our enemies," Mendoza said and repeated his words to be certain that the cacique understood. "The animals are very thin now." He held up one finger to show how thin they were. "They are thin because many moons have gone since we have had enemies to kill."

Chief Tlascingo pointed to himself, to those around him, to the houses huddled at the far end of the plaza, where women and children were hiding from us.

"In Tawhi," he said, "here everyone is a friend."

"This I observe and make note of," Mendoza replied.

From time to time while the two men were talking, Tlascingo had stolen a glance at Mendoza's matchlock and at the crossbow I carried. He now asked about them.

Mendoza handed over his heavy weapon and showed the cacique how to aim it, but, thinking of our lack of powder, did not allow him to fire. Instead, he clapped his hands and made a loud sound to imitate an explosion.

"It speaks with the voice of thunder," Mendoza explained.

"With a loud tongue," the cacique said.

"With the tongue of thunder."

"Against your enemies?"

"Against them only," said Mendoza.

He then took the crossbow and from my quiver a quarrel feathered with boar's hair. Slowly turning the ratchet, he spanned the bow and aimed at a wall three times the distance the cacique could reach with an arrow. The quarrel sped on its way, thudded into the mud wall, and buried itself so deeply that a youth sent to retrieve the iron bolt could not dig it out.

"Also against our enemies," Mendoza said, holding up the crossbow. "Those who have evil hearts and speak from crooked mouths."

This act at an end, Mendoza took from his doublet a small deerskin pouch filled with gold dust and nuggets he had gathered in Nexpan, which Torres had not stolen because the Captain wore it around his neck as a charm. On the ground Zia laid out a row of glass bangles, necklaces, thin bracelets of Toledo steel, and other oddments.

Mendoza emptied the gold into his hand. "For this I will trade what lies before you."

The cacique's eyes lighted up, though they were deep-set and almost hidden by a bang of hair, coarse as a horse's tail. A jerk of his head sent two men running off across the plaza, to return shortly with a small pouch.

In the past Tlascingo had spent many years at the business of barter, if I can judge from what now went on. And among those tribes with whom he bartered, he must have gained a wily reputation. No matter how Mendoza tried, with patience or without, no trinket brought more than ten pinches of dust (with thumb and forefinger the cacique himself did the pinching). Many brought less. Indeed, so clever was the cacique, that by late afternoon the trinkets were gone and all Mendoza had gained were some thirty *onzas* of gold.

From his doublet Mendoza then drew forth four well-worn gaming cards — a deuce of coins, a seven of cups, a *caballero* of swords, a *sota* of cups — and placed them in a row at the cacique's feet.

"These," he said, "for the gold that remains."

Tlascingo grunted. "Half," he said.

Mendoza picked up three cards and put them away, leaving the *caballero* of swords.

It was the fairest card of all, bordered green and yellow, with a fierce-eyed *hidalgo* astride a rearing stallion. It caught the cacique's fancy. He stooped and from his deerskin bag drew out a dozen careful pinches of gold, placing them on the card. But Mendoza in disgust turned his back.

After a long silence the cacique added three pinches to the pile.

Mendoza held up two fingers. "More," he said.

Tlascingo did not move. Shadows lengthened, the sun began to sink below the cliffs of Tawhi. Still the cacique stood with folded arms, as if he might stand there forever.

At last Mendoza poured the gold into his bag, and handed the prized card to Tlascingo.

"Tomorrow," the cacique said, looking well pleased with himself, "we bargain again. Now I take you to a place where you can rest."

The place was nearby, a windowless hut without furnishings, and a dirt floor covered with corn husks.

"When the sun is gone my men will give you food," Tlascingo said. "Tomorrow we bargain again."

"Tomorrow," Mendoza said, "bring a large bag of gold.

179

The card you have is of less value than the others." He then asked a bold question. "Whence comes this gold, mighty Tlascingo?"

"From far mountains," Tlascingo answered.

"Much?"

"Gold to last my life and the life of my son and the life of his son and the life of his son," the cacique said, boastfully.

"If you possess gold in these quantities, why do you measure it out in pinches?"

"I do so because it pleases me. If I wish I could give you more gold than you can carry. More than your animals with the long tails can carry."

"This I will remember," Mendoza broke in. "Tomorrow when you offer a dozen thin pinches for a thing that is worth the weight of a man."

Tlascingo started to speak, but paused, aware perhaps that he had gone too far in his boasts. Then a second thought passed swiftly across his face. Suspiciously he glanced at the crossbow and the weapon which made a noise like thunder.

"I keep little gold in my storehouse," he said. "The gold is far away."

"Where?" Mendoza asked.

"In the mountains," the cacique answered, making a sweeping movement of his hand that took in the east, the south, the north. "In a mountain known only to six of my warriors. Those who gather it there are prisoners I have captured in battle. The prisoners are blind. I blinded them so they cannot tell my secret."

180

He looked straight at Mendoza for a moment and without further speech walked away.

I wondered what use Tlascingo had for all the gold he boasted about. He could not use it in barter, for the Indians we had met on our journeys did not value it. The answer to my question was soon forthcoming.

# 22

THE CACIQUE LEFT BEHIND two of his retainers, young men of serious mien who seated themselves on either side of the doorway. Whether they were there to care for our wants or to guard us, we did not know. But when we went out into the plaza, after making a brief survey of our new abode, they did not follow.

"I have an idea that Tlascingo's storehouse is filled with gold," Mendoza said. "Heaped up from floor to roof."

Father Francisco with his cross was walking ahead of us, out of earshot.

"But how do we lay our hands on it?" he continued.

"Or carry it down from the mountain, if we do," I said, though the thought of stealing Tlascingo's gold was far from my mind.

"Perhaps it is stored in deerskin bags, like the one the Indians brought from the storehouse. They were scarcely gone long enough to fill a bag. Bags of gold we could toss down over the cliff."

"Easily," I said, not serious about the matter. "One bag after another."

"I watched the two men Tlascingo sent for the gold,"

Mendoza said. "I saw where they went. The doorway they entered. It is just beyond the place where the spring comes forth."

We crossed the plaza, stopping for a drink at the spring. But as we came to the storehouse Mendoza did not pause nor look through the doorway, though he let me know in a whisper which one it was.

"We will have a look on the way back," he said.

Leisurely we strolled to the far end of the plaza, past sheds where corn was stored and ground, a large open room in which several old women were weaving, where Zia and Father Francisco left us. Slowly we returned along the way we had come. The two young men still sat against the wall of our hut, apparently not watching us.

"Here it is," Mendoza said. "Walk to the spring and do not look back. I will be with you in a moment."

I did as I was told and by the time I reached the spring Mendoza overtook me.

"A small room," he said. "With no windows and only the one door. In the center of the room is a pile of gold, fine as dust, but no more than would fill a helmet or two."

"No bags?"

"None."

We drank again from the spring and then followed a well-worn path which led toward the lake.

"The floor is covered over with a sprinkling of gold," Mendoza said. "Which means that at some time the small pile was a large pile. Gold must have filled the store-house."

We had reached a stone terrace that ran for a dozen

*varas* along the marge of the lake. From it there was a fine view of a mesa below us and a half-circle of dark mountains beyond.

Mendoza said, "If Tlascingo's gold comes from far off, we could search a year and not find the place. But what if we camped on the mesa? Somewhere out of sight, where we could see anyone coming from the mountains or going to them? We might surprise Tlascingo's men with a load of gold. Or trail them to where it is being mined."

I heard most of what he said, but my thoughts were on the surpassing scene that lay before me. The mountains changing from purple to black. The clouds that rose above them lighted by the fires of sunset. The shadowed mesa rolling away in all directions. The city itself and the rock it was built upon afloat together in the sky, like a great ship.

Yet as Mendoza talked and I stood looking down at the beauty before me, wondering how I could capture it all in a map, I suddenly remembered the gold nugget, bigger than a chestnut, that I had found in Nexpan. And again, as it had before, the curious fever, the sickness seized me.

Mendoza was pointing northward. "About halfway between us and yonder tall peak you can see a stream," he said. "One bend of it where it makes a circle around a wooded hill. We could travel there by night, camp on the far side, and use the hill as a lookout."

"Tlascingo," I said, "is no fool. When we leave here he will have us followed, until we are well out of his country."

"Perhaps. It is the chance we take. But we have little

to lose. Here there is nothing for us, since we have only three cards and a piece of mirror to barter with."

"We have mules," I said. "Tlascingo would trade all the gold in his storehouse for a mule."

"It is against the King's law."

"The law forbids the sale or gift of a horse. It does not speak of mules."

"Are you certain?"

"Certain."

"Then, Estéban, you have an interesting idea. We will barter one mule for all the gold it can carry."

Reaching the end of the terrace, we turned to retrace our steps. For the first time I noticed that a lively spring poured forth from a cleft rock in the center of the terrace and fell tinkling into the lake from a stone in the shape of a serpent's mouth. Beside this figure was a low bench or platform carved of stone. From it steps led downward to the lake in winding, snakelike curves.

"Something takes place here," I said. "A ceremony."

Mendoza, deep in thought, did not answer.

The surface of the lake was smooth as a shield. At the far end, where the cliff dropped away into air, clouds were mirrored. Nearer at hand the water was clear and I could see small fish darting about. As I watched them I became aware that the water cast up an unusual light. It is a reflection of the evening sky, I thought. Yet when I looked closer I saw that the light came not from above but from below, from the very bottom of the lake.

I grasped Mendoza's arm. "Have you seen that color before? Under the water, there on the bottom."

Mendoza stared long into the depths of the lake, glanced at the sky and then back into the depths.

"I have seen it before," he said quietly.

"At Nexpan?"

"Yes, there. In the sand of the stream."

We looked at each other.

"It is the color of gold," I said.

"It *is* gold," Mendoza whispered. "The bottom of the lake is solid gold."

Darkness fell as we stood there speechless, staring into the depths of the lake. The startled cry of a waterfowl, the sound of a breaking twig brought us to our senses. We turned and hastily groped our way back along the path.

The plaza was ringed with evening fires. The smell of piñon smoke and roasting meat hung heavy in the air. The two young men were nowhere in sight. Through the doorway of our hut I could see Father Francisco and Zia sitting beside a small fire.

Mendoza stopped outside. "Tell the dear Father nothing," he said. "Speak no word of what we have beheld. And think with all your wits. While you are eating, think. Think also while you sleep. For there exists some way that we can dredge up that golden reef." His tongue trembled with excitement. "A thousand hundred-weight lies there beneath the water, waiting to be taken. But how? How? If only I had ten armed men. Or five!"

Our supper, brought by the young Indians, was plentiful, of deer meat in thick slabs, and parched cornmeal mixed with deer fat, but Mendoza and I ate little. After the meal was over we walked outside.

"Have you thought of anything?" he asked.

"Of nothing," I answered. I did not speak what I really thought — that any plan to capture the gold was doomed to fail, and that it was madness to try. "Nothing," I repeated.

"You are one who observes things," he said. "The height of a mountain, the way a river runs, a bird's color. Tell me, how is the lake situated? Does it lie higher than the plaza and the city?"

"Four or five *varas* higher. Remember that we climbed a flight of steps to reach the terrace. And the terrace is only a *vara* above the surface of the lake."

"Therefore, the lake is not natural. It has been made by hand."

"Perhaps in the beginning there was a hollow place in the rock between the spring and the edge of the cliff, which is the higher of the two. Someone had the idea of making the lake larger, so they built a dam behind the spring and thus backed up the water."

"Then it is the terrace that serves as a dam."

"No," I said, "the dam is made of earth. There are small trees, bushes, and grass growing on it. The terrace is of rocks set together. A sort of capping to keep the earth from washing away."

"Now that you speak of it, I remember the trees and the grass. What is the thickness of the dam, do you say?"

"Six *varas*."

"At the base of the dam?"

"There it might be thicker."

Mendoza asked no more questions as he stood there with his eyes on the lake, but I knew what he was thinking.

The lake formed by the earthen dam was a third the size of the whole city. If somehow the dam could be breached, the water would rush out, down upon the city in a roaring flood, sweeping everything before it, leaving the gold exposed.

The moon rose. It made a pathway across the lake.

"I have a plan," Mendoza said.

He did not need to tell me what it was.

# 23

I<small>N THE MORNING</small> I awakened to the sweet-sounding note of a horn. The horn blew again and I heard the murmur of voices, the shuffle of feet, and as I sat up saw a young Indian in the doorway, beckoning to me.

I shook Mendoza awake. Dressing hurriedly, we followed the Indian, one of the two young men who had sat outside our hut the day before, across the deserted plaza. Against the paling sky, on the terrace above the lake, stood a group of robed figures.

"A ceremony to the sun," Mendoza whispered.

"Different from Nexpan," I answered.

"Like the one in Peru," Mendoza said. "The one Torres talks about."

The Indian led the way along a path that circled the terrace and silently left us. We found ourselves among a growth of pines near the lake's edge, partly hidden yet with a good view of the terrace and the robed figures.

The cacique stood apart, beside the stone serpent from whose mouth water ran forth into the lake. He was naked except for a clout and a plumed headdress. Behind him

189

hovered retainers, and on both sides, filling the terrace, were his subjects, the Indians of Tawhi.

The sun burst from the plain and, as at Nexpan, a cry of exultation rose from the crowd. From Torres and the word of travelers in the country of Peru, I had heard tales of a golden god, but to see him take shape there before our eyes was a magic I shall never forget.

Into gourds filled with glistening oil, retainers dipped their hands and ran them over Tlascingo's body and his face, even the bottoms of his feet. Other retainers stepped forward and with gourds, like giant salt cellars, sprinkled him over with fine dust, until he was a figure of gold, bright as the sun itself.

Tlascingo raised his arms to the east. While the crowd chanted, he went majestically down the steps and into the lake, far out, until only his face and plumed headdress could be seen above the water. There his retainers, who had followed at a distance, overtook him and washed his body free of gold. Then lifting the cacique, they threw a feathered cloak about his shoulders and triumphantly carried him back to the terrace.

"Thus," whispered Mendoza, "has come the gold that paves the lake. Through the centuries, from the bodies of countless caciques."

I doubt that he saw much of the ceremony. For whenever I glanced at him his eyes were turned to the dam, measuring its height and thickness and slope, fixing the whole thing in his mind. It was frightening to know and to see clearly by daylight, that his mad scheme was possible.

In mid-morning, Mendoza began to trade with the cacique. It did not last long. He made a show of bargaining, so as not to arouse suspicion, but by noon we were on our way down from the mountain. Before we left, Mendoza promised that he would return after two suns had gone.

"To the east," Mendoza said, "there are many Spaniards." This was said to warn the cacique that if he attacked our small band he would have to answer to an army. "From them I will get many things to trade. I will also bring with me, to the foot of your ladder if possible, one of our animals, a gentle one, which I will also trade for the gold it can carry on its back."

The cacique's face brightened. He pointed to the gilded cuirass that Mendoza wore. "The little house you live in," he said, "you will bring one of these, too?"

"Yes," said Mendoza and he stepped back, inviting the cacique to shoot an arrow at him, which the cacique did. As the arrow struck the armor and bounded harmlessly away, Mendoza said, "I will bring a little house like this one, an animal, and many things to barter. In two suns, I will bring them."

Mendoza had promised to return in two days because this was the time needed to make more pouches with which to transport the cacique's gold. In our winter camp we had killed deer and the hides we had cured and carried away with us, hoping to put them to good use.

At our hidden camp below, we now set to work on these hides, working from dawn until darkness and then by firelight. The pouches were sewn tight at the seams, since the Tawhi gold was dustlike. They were made to hold an *arroba,* the weight Mendoza deemed one man could easily carry.

My part of the task I did without enthusiasm and therefore poorly. One of the bags I was finishing Mendoza took from me and held to the light.

"This will not hold dust," he said. "I doubt that it will hold rocks." He tossed it into my lap. "You do not like the making of bags?"

"I am not a wielder of thread and needle," I answered.

"Neither is Roa nor the others, but they do twice the work." A suspicious glint showed in his eyes. "Perhaps," he said, lowering his voice so that Father Francisco and Zia would not hear him, "there is another reason why you work slowly and what you do is bad. Is it that you are not pleased with my plan?"

"I am not pleased."

"Why?"

"Because it is dangerous."

"What, *señor,* is not dangerous? Have we not breakfasted on danger? Nooned and dined upon danger? Is not every moment lived in danger? You are no coward, though you are a young man of great timidity. There is a difference between the two. Tell me, you must have another reason."

"The plan is dangerous," I repeated. "To us and likewise to the Indians of Tawhi."

Mendoza laughed. He looked at Roa and Roa laughed, too.

"Our comrade worries about the Indians," he said.

"Let me tell him about Tlascingo. He owns a lake whose bottom is covered with gold. It is thicker than the thickest carpet. Thicker than the cobbles that pave the streets of Seville. We dig a hole through the dam. Out runs the water."

"You dig a hole in the dam?"

"A tunnel."

"You will drown in any tunnel you dig below the surface of the lake."

"Perhaps a trough, a channel across the terrace," Mendoza said. "Do you think this would be better?"

I did not answer.

"When the channel is dug," he said, "out runs the water."

"Where does the water run to?" I asked, as if I did not know.

"It runs across the plaza and through the houses, which have nothing in them except a few pots. It runs out and over the cliff."

"When the water runs across the plaza and through the houses, what happens to the people?"

"They scramble to the roof tops, of course."

"The young ones and the old?"

"All of them. For all are nimble as goats, else they would not live on a crag. And as they sit on the roofs we shovel gold and fill the bags."

"Those on the roof tops," I said, "what do they do while you fill the bags?"

"They sit."

"And do nothing?"

"No, they sit and think of the weapon which makes the noise of thunder. The shaft that sinks itself so deep that it cannot be found. Of the little iron houses that protect us from their stones and arrows. Of the army waiting behind us. They think of these and do nothing."

"The people have courage, like those at Háwikuh."

"Also, they have much gold," Mendoza said. "Enough there at the bottom of the lake to burden the backs of a thousand mules. Do you think that they will risk their lives because we take a few bags? And remember, *hidalgo,* the mine, of which the cacique boasted, so rich that a hundred years will not exhaust it!"

Mendoza went on, speaking quietly but in a sort of frenzy. At last, aware that he could not change my mind, he shrugged his shoulders and walked away.

On the second afternoon, when the bags were finished, Mendoza scoured the camp for things he could trade to Tlascingo — an iron bar, a worn-out surcingle, a shirt lacking buttons, a mirror of Zuñiga's, which he broke into five pieces. These he packed each in a separate bag. The rest of the bags he divided in two parts, stuffing one within the other, to make it seem that he brought many things to barter.

At dawn he made four bundles and wrapped the digging tools in a hide. He then called me away, out of the hearing of Zia and Father Francisco.

"I leave you with the animals," he said. "For you are better here than on the mountain. See that they are watered. And have them ready at sunrise tomorrow. Pack saddles. Everything."

"I understand."

"And take care that you say nothing to Zia or Father Francisco. Is all of this clear, *señor?*"

"Yes."

"May you go with God."

"And may you, also," I said.

But as the two men left the camp and went up the trail with the bags and implements loaded on a mule, I said to myself, "I shall never in this life see them again."

# 24

WAITED while Roa and Mendoza climbed the ladder and disappeared into the Cloud City. Then I went to the meadow where the animals were tethered and curried each one, except the colt.

As I worked, taking most of the morning to do the task, I made my plans for the next day. I decided that before dawn I would break camp, pack all of our baggage, and when the sun rose have the train ready beside the cliff. If by mid-morning the men had not come down from the mountain, I would leave and travel east until nightfall. There we would stay for two days. Then, if the men did not appear, I would go on to Háwikuh by the trail we had broken.

Near noon, as I started back to camp with the train, Zia came running through the trees. Her eyes were fixed on the animals plodding along behind me.

"Where is Blue Star?" she cried.

"In the meadow, grazing."

"You have combed the others, I see."

"And Blue Star also," I said to tease her. Never a day passed that she did not curry the colt. This was her task and no one dared to undertake it. "She was in need of the comb," I explained.

"I combed her yesterday."

"Not well."

Her eyes took fire and she scolded me in the language of Nayarit. Whenever she was angry, forgetting her Spanish, she always spoke to me in this outlandish tongue.

Zia had changed. She was not a child any more. In the six months or so between winter and spring, she had become a young woman. She was no longer all arms and legs and awkward movements, but filled out, more graceful, and more serious.

I think there was a moment, an exact time, when she put her childhood behind. It was on the trail moving away from our winter camp on a spring day. We had passed a nest of twigs and leaves, into which at our passing a half-dozen or more creatures much like her aguatil had scurried. Returning to the nest, she took Montezuma from her pocket, and with a little ceremony, set him on the ground, said something under her breath, and left.

The mules went by as she spoke. Blue Star, recognizing her voice, came trotting up the path. The colt understood Nayarit better than I did, for she spoke to it only in that language. If she had not, still the colt would have understood more than I. Words of the Nayarit country make a soft hissing sound, like steam in a pot.

In a glance Zia saw that the colt had not been combed that day. She fell silent and a small smile hovered around her lips. Yet I knew that she was not ready to forgive the teasing.

"Look," I said in the tone of a conspirator. "I have been thinking a big thought. All day it has been tumbling around in my head."

She had snatched up a handful of grass and flowers and was about to feed it to the colt. She paused but did not look at me.

I walked over to the colt and threw a halter around its neck.

"Today," I said, "you ride Blue Star."

Zia stepped back. Her eyes grew large. She took another step backward.

"The Captain has forbidden it," she said. "Many times I have asked him."

"The Captain is not here. Nor Roa. Only Father Francisco and he will say nothing."

Zia cast a frightened look over her shoulder, as if she expected to see Mendoza bearing down upon us.

I brought the colt to where she stood and cupped my two hands into a stirrup.

"Your foot, *señorita.*"

Slowly she put out her foot, the wrong one. She was trembling.

"The left foot, young lady. Or else you will ride facing the rear."

She changed feet and with a quick thrust I boosted her to Blue Star's back. I grasped the halter, which was looped over my arm. Mendoza and Roa had taken turns that spring at breaking the colt, yet I was not certain what would happen. The forest around was thick with pine needles. If she falls, I thought, it will be upon a soft bed.

To my surprise the two walked off together, girl and colt, as if this were the way it had been always. I walked along beside them, ready if Blue Star took the notion to stand on her hind legs or to lie down or bolt through the trees.

"Give me the halter," Zia said, after a short distance.

With misgivings I handed it up. "Watch for the limbs of trees," I warned her. "Hold tight and do not trot. Recall that you are not yet a *vaquera*."

We had nearly reached the camp, without mishap, when Zia slid down from the colt's back. She held the reins and walked to where I stood admiring her. On her toes, she reached up and, to my immense surprise, kissed me on the cheek.

"Before you ride again," I said to cover my embarrassment, "help me with the cross-staff."

"But I helped you yesterday," she replied, holding tight to the halter. "Since we have not traveled anywhere, why do you need to use it again?"

"Yesterday's reading may be wrong," I said and fetched the cross-staff from the case she had made for me.

Zia had helped me many times on the trail and was now expert at this difficult task. Holding one end of the staff on her shoulder, she stood, scarcely breathing, while I placed the peepholes in line with the sun and the horizon.

"May I ride away now?" she asked.

Usually, she waited until I had made the notations.

I helped her into the saddle and she set off along the

path we had just traveled. This time she rode without grasping the colt's mane. With her free hand, she waved to me. I have never seen anyone so happy. If I had not told her to return in time to help me with the baggage, I believe that she would have ridden until dark.

# 25

**M**Y READING with the cross-staff proved to be the same as the one I had taken the day before, and with it I laid out what I thought would be a shorter route to Háwikuh. I spent the afternoon doing this. At dusk I watered the animals and laid out the pack saddles, ready for morning.

When I reached camp, dusk was deepening into night. It was the hour when the two men would be in their hut, waiting for darkness.

Zia and Father Francisco had roasted a rabbit in the pit, which the three of us ate with fried corncakes. As I sat beside the fire I thought, this is the time Roa and Mendoza have begun to dig the channel across the top of the dam. They take turns, one pushing the earth aside while the other loosens it with spade and bar. They work fast, pausing to listen, talking in whispers. I could see them clearly, as clearly as if I were there on the mountain.

Father Francisco was talking about the people of Tawhi, and how he hoped to save many of their souls.

"They are like the people of Nexpan," he said. "Devout but misguided. Tomorrow I will go again to talk to them and raise the cross I have spent this day in making.

They are stubborn, yet I will wear them down."

"Tomorrow," I said, "we leave Tawhi."

He looked across the fire, cocking his head to one side, like a bird.

"By whose command?" he asked.

"By the command of Captain Mendoza."

"He said nothing to me."

"I am sorry, Father, it is my fault. He told me to tell you that we are leaving. But I forgot. In the morning he and Roa return. Everything is to be ready. That is the command."

Father Francisco fell silent. In a short time, he rose and hobbled off to bed, mumbling to himself. Zia, exhausted by excitement and the five leagues she must have ridden back and forth, followed him.

I walked out from the trees. The air was clear and the moon had not risen. The fires of Tawhi glowed against the darksome sky.

I went to where the animals were tethered and tried the picket ropes. Everything was secure. I stretched out in the grass, but did not sleep.

The moon came up. It was the shape of a bitter orange and pale gold. By its light, I thought, the men will be able to work faster. They have been digging for more than two hours. The channel, wide as a man's body, now must be a fourth of the way through the earthen dam.

The fires of Tawhi grew faint and died and the stars above the mountain shone bright, red Antares in particular, and two small stars in the Scorpion's tail.

I dozed, but not long, for Antares had moved no more

than the breadth of a finger. It was very quiet. From the mountain I heard the barking of a dog. Mendoza and Roa hear the barking, too, I thought. They have stopped their work and are listening.

Minutes went by, but the dog did not bark again.

"The men have gone back to work," I said to myself. "They dig faster now, to make up the time lost."

The two small stars in the tail of Scorpion disappeared behind the mountain. A chill came into the air and dew began to cover the grass. I threw more wood onto the fire and went again to look at the animals. From somewhere near a wolf coyote called. From far off it was answered. I was tired yet I dared not lie down for fear of falling asleep.

Faint light showed along the horizon. Quietly, I began to saddle the train, taking care that the pack frames sat evenly and secure. From time to time I looked up at the mountain. All was dark and quiet.

The first breakfast fire showed on the mountain. Now the time is near, I thought. It was still a half hour before sunrise, but the men would not wait much longer. I stood away from the trees, where I had a better view of the mountain, the houses, and the western cliff rising sheer to meet them.

The horizon grew brighter. The Indians of Tawhi would soon be leaving their homes, walking across the plaza and up the terrace to the lake.

I watched the cliff and the houses huddled on its edge. Minutes passed. It is too late now, I thought, already the Indians have left their homes and are on their way to the lake. Yet, it is possible that this is the very moment Mendoza has waited for.

Suddenly, the thought came to me that something had gone wrong with their plans. Had they been attacked as they worked there on the terrace? Unmindful of my warning, had Mendoza tried to dig a tunnel through the dam and been trapped by a fall of earth or rushing water? With such a mad scheme, many things could go amiss.

Above me and seemingly from a long distance, as if it came from the sky itself, I heard a sound. It was like the soughing of a strong wind or the movement of great wings. The sound did not come from the sky, but from the mountain. It was no longer the sound of wings or wind, but a roar.

The roar grew. As I stood transfixed, a plume of white water broke from the mountain, hung in the bright morning air, and fell sparkling to earth.

I ran through the forest and, gathering the pack train, set off toward the cliff. Zia and Father Francisco stood awestruck beside the fire, but I passed them without speaking. I rode up the trail to where it ended in a pile of rocks, some fifty paces from the cliff and the dangling ladder.

By the time I had dismounted, turned the train around, and faced each animal down the trail, the first bag of gold had fallen. It lay at the foot of the cliff in a grassy swale. A second, a third bag thudded into the grass, as I was loading the first. I saw Roa standing on the cliff. He waved and disappeared.

Above me, not a sound came from the City of Clouds.

*The Fortress of San Juan de Ulúa*
*Vera Cruz, in New Spain*
*The tenth day of October*
*The year of our Lord's birth, 1541*

THE SEA IS CALM after the storm. As we cross the parapet on our way to the courtroom it lies around us gentle as a lake. But across the bay I see rows of palms along the shore of Vera Cruz, cut down by the wind. We walk fast, Don Felipe and I. The sun is overhead and the stones of the parapet burn through our boots.

Don Felipe says, "You remember the little speech we have rehearsed?"

"Each word."

"And remember this, also," he says. "Talk slowly, when you talk. Look at the judges and not, as is your custom, at your feet. Let your manner be courteous. Do not forget that when there is no honey in the jar, it is wise to have some in the mouth."

"Torres," I say, speaking what is most in my thoughts, "have you seen him?"

"No, but from what others tell me, he is a rattlehead."

"A thief," I say. "A stealer of horses."

"Thief or rattlehead or both, let this be of no comfort to you. Torres is not the one who is on trial. He is a wit-

205

ness, brought here by the royal fiscal from a far distance, to prove you guilty of murder. Whatever he says, therefore, will be listened to by the Audiencia as if he were the Archbishop of Córdoba himself."

"This I fear most."

"This I fear, too, but we will give the rattlehead some thought," Don Felipe says as we enter the courtroom, "after we hear his testimony."

I look for Torres in the crowded room, but do not see him. The three judges are there in their rusty black robes. More than ever they remind me of the three black *zopilotes* on the ruined wall at Chichilticale. The room is stifling hot and again the robes are tucked up over their bony knees. Today an Indian boy stands behind them, pulling at a cord which is fastened to a large palm leaf.

The royal fiscal approaches me as I stand in front of the three judges.

I have forgotten what he says at first. In any event, it is not important. Shuffling through his papers, he pauses briefly to read one of them. He gathers the papers into a neat roll and reaching out with it, taps me lightly on the chest.

"You have testified," he says, "that the treasure found by Captain Mendoza in Cíbola required twelve animals to transport."

The courtroom grows quiet.

"That the treasure amounted to some sixty thousand *onzas* of the purest gold. That when you left a place called Nexpan you carried with you only enough gold to fill two helmets."

I listen to the royal fiscal, but I am thinking about Guillermo Torres. He is somewhere in the courtroom. I glance around, everywhere except behind me. At last I see him or someone who looks much like him.

"Am I correct?" the fiscal says. "Have you testified to these facts?"

"I have, sir."

Yes, it is Torres. He is sitting beside the window, almost hidden by one of the notaries. I can just see his head over the notary's shoulder, the puffy face and bulging eyes.

"Now I would like to know," the fiscal says, "how the two helmets of gold became a hoard which only many beasts could carry. Tell us, *señor,* how this came about."

"The helmets of gold did not become a hoard," I answer. Raising my hand I point straight at Torres, the thief. "For the reason that this man, Guillermo Torres, stole them from us while we slept."

The royal fiscal waves the roll of papers above his head. He shouts something at me, yet I go on.

"While we were encamped near the City of Nexpan, he, Guillermo Torres, stole the gold and our best horse, and fled."

Onlookers crane their necks to get a view of the man I have pointed out. But Torres, like a turtle, draws in his head and is suddenly hidden behind the notary.

One of the judges warns me against further outbursts, and the fiscal, still waving the papers, adds a word of his own.

"It is you who are on trial, not Señor Torres," he says,

repeating what Don Felipe already has told me. "Kindly, therefore, answer the question asked of you."

My counsel rises to speak for me, but is told by one of the judges to be seated.

After a moment or two, when I have controlled myself, I begin the story of our arrival in the City of Tawhi. I tell how we discovered gold in the lake and how it got there. I am careful not to say that the lake bottom was covered deep with it. Nevertheless, the fiscal interrupts me.

"The gold at the bottom of the lake," he says. "From whence did it come?"

"From a mine far distant in the mountains," I answer. "Its location we never learned."

"How much gold did the lake yield?"

I answer his question truthfully. "The gold we carried away."

I glance beyond the fiscal to where Torres sits, still hidden from sight, as though he would rather be any other place than in this courtroom. For the first time it occurs to me that he may be here against his will. If so, then what I have said against him is a mistake.

"Continue," the fiscal says sharply.

I gather my thoughts and do as I am bidden. I tell the Audiencia of Mendoza's scheme for seizing the treasure. How the scheme was secretly carried out in the night, and of the dawn when I stood below the mountain and watched the unloosed lake pour over the cliff.

"You were not with Captain Mendoza?" the fiscal says.

"No, sir."

"Where were you?"

"In camp."

"Below the mountain?"

"Yes, below."

"Why there and not with Captain Mendoza?" the fiscal asks. "Was it because he did not trust you?"

"Someone was needed to tend the animals."

"As I understand it, there were two others in the party. A priest, Father Francisco. And Zia Troyano, a guide. Why could they not tend the animals?"

I am surprised that he knows Zia's name. Truly, the Royal Audiencia is thorough. It is as thorough as the *Suprema* and the Grand Inquisitor.

"Speak!" the fiscal commands me.

"The priest was lame. Zia Troyano is a girl."

"But they could have tended the animals, and you could have helped with the tunnel, if Captain Mendoza had not mistrusted you."

I say nothing.

The fiscal looks at the papers.

"We know from your testimony," he says, "from your last appearance before the Audiencia, that you and Captain Mendoza quarreled over the gold found at Nexpan."

"There was no quarrel," I break in. "And so I testified."

I remember because the day I testified to this I carefully wrote down my words. And only this morning I have looked at them again.

The fiscal goes on as if he had not heard me. "We shall prove that bad blood between Captain Mendoza and the defendant, which existed at Nexpan and at Tawhi, led to the death of Captain Mendoza at the hands of the defendant."

He turns his back upon me, and in a loud voice calls Guillermo Torres to stand before the Audiencia.

I sit down beside my counsel. Torres leaves the corner and takes his place before the three judges. He keeps his eyes on the floor, even when he swears upon the Cross.

The fiscal asks his name, the name of his birthplace, his occupation, the length of time he knew Captain Mendoza. To all these questions, Torres gives slow answers, while he shifts about. More than ever, I am certain that he is here against his will. My counsel thinks likewise. We are wrong. He is here to get his hands on the treasure, if he can.

"Now," the fiscal says, "will you tell the Royal Audiencia about the quarrel between Captain Mendoza and the defendant? How it began?"

"It began while they were away in Nexpan," Torres replies. "So I did not see the beginning. But when they came out of the Abyss and I was waiting there with the mules and horses, the Captain and Father Francisco were arguing. The argument went on for a while just between the two of them. Then Estéban there" (Torres pauses and for the first time casts a glance in my direction), "Estéban took the side of Father Francisco and the three of them argued. Then Father Francisco walked away and the others argued together."

So far Torres, the thief, has spoken untruthfully.

"Did Estéban de Sandoval threaten Captain Mendoza?"

the fiscal asks. "Did he say at this time, 'Someday I shall kill you?' "

Quiet falls upon the courtroom. Everyone is listening, even the three judges. There is no sound except the rustle of the big palm leaf as the Indian boy pulls it up and down, up and down.

Torres shows no surprise at the fiscal's question. "He has heard the question before," my counsel whispers. "He has been waiting for the fiscal to ask it."

Torres looks at the judges and says, "I was standing about ten paces from them by the fire and I saw Estéban raise his fist and say this."

"Say what?" the fiscal prompts him.

" 'Someday I shall kill you!' "

Anger seizes me. I rise to my feet, but the counsel grasps my arm and forces me back.

" 'Someday I shall kill you,' " the fiscal says. "You heard these words spoken clearly?"

"Yes, clearly."

Slowly the fiscal walks to the table and pours himself a drink of water. Slowly he walks back and takes his position in front of the three judges.

"Now, Señor Torres," he says, "Captain Mendoza and the *conducta* went on for several days. Tell the Audiencia what happened during these travels."

"We went on," Torres says, "for two days, I think. And then a storm came and we took shelter in a cave and waited for good weather."

"While you waited in the cave, did Estéban de Sandoval

211

again threaten Captain Mendoza's life?"

"I did not hear the threats."

"There could have been threats that you did not hear?"

"Yes, sir."

"You left the cave after a few days and returned to Háwikuh alone. Why?"

"Because," Torres says, "I did not want to stay with men who were fighting."

"Was there another reason for leaving?"

"Yes. They had promised me a share of the gold, but I did not receive it."

"Continue, Señor Torres."

"When I did not receive the gold from them, I took what was my rightful share and left and rode back to Háwikuh."

Lies, all lies! I sit listening to each one, helpless, silent. My counsel says for me to wait until he questions Torres, then things will be different. But when he does, it is the same. The lies are spoken again. Torres does not change his story by so much as a word.

My own story, which the counsel asks me to tell, sounds flat as it comes from my mouth. There is no air in the courtroom. The fan moves up and down, yet no air stirs. Light from the sea casts gray shadows on the faces of the three judges. Behind me I can hear whispers, the shuffle of feet, and, very far somewhere, the tolling of a church bell.

As I finish the story of Torres' theft, the fiscal rises and says to the judges, "The defendant is excused. I do not wish to question him." He says it with indifference, as if anything I might answer would be of no importance to him or to anyone.

At this point my counsel takes the notes I have put together and gives them to the fiscal, who does not look at them. He tosses the notes on the table in front of the judges but makes no comment.

"I ask," he says, "that the trial be adjourned for two days, until the twelfth day of October. At that time I will present an item of written evidence. And a second witness."

Thus ends this day before the Royal Audiencia, a day that has not gone well for me.

My legs feel weak and my head is giddy as Don Felipe and I cross the parapet on our way to the cell. The sun rests heavily on my back, like a hot stone. It is the stone of Sisyphus which I carry upon my back.

"What," I ask, "is the written evidence the fiscal spoke about?"

"That I do not know," Don Felipe answers. "But the witness I have news of."

I wait for Don Felipe to continue. We pass the cells where the prisoners stand because they cannot sit and he pauses to inquire if everyone is in good health. He is greeted by silence. He has forgotten what he started to say. He is thinking about the map I make for him, on what day it will be finished, what he will then do with it, the treasure he will find.

"The witness," I say.

"Oh, the witness, the one the fiscal mentioned. It is the guide, Zia Troyano."

"Zia?"

The sun suddenly bursts into a thousand pieces and the stone terrace seems to melt beneath my feet.

The cell is quiet. Don Felipe has been here to see how the map progresses. He has left now on his evening rounds, satisfied with what I have done. In appearance it is a good map, yet with it he will never find the treasure.

The star shines wanly in the west. I must go on and tell the story of our journey from Tawhi, the Cloud City, of the death of Captain Mendoza and the evil it brought. But how do I ever write this down when my head whirls around and around, when all I can think of is Zia Troyano?

# 26

BEFORE THE SUN stood three hours high, all of us working at the task except Zia and Father Francisco, the pack train was loaded with the bags Roa had tossed down from the cliff, and we had left the Cloud City and the forest far behind.

We rode hard and warily until noon, in corselet and helmet, though there was no sign that the Indians followed us. Then beside the stream we halted to rest the animals and adjust the bags, which in our haste to leave Tawhi had not been properly balanced.

I was surprised at Roa and Mendoza. They were grimy with dirt, but seemed as fresh as if they had slept all night. I was curious to know what had happened to them on the mountain, and here as we rested beside the stream Roa told me. It was not the same story that Mendoza told Father Francisco.

"We traded with the cacique until dark," Roa said. "He was very pleased with the trading, for Mendoza planned it that way. He kept making signs about the mule that Mendoza had promised to barter, but Mendoza made signs back that he would have to wait until morning."

Roa paused and glanced around to see that Father Francisco was not within hearing. The priest had said nothing when Mendoza explained to him that once each year the lake was emptied in order to retrieve the gold, and that the bags he had tossed over the cliff he had bargained for.

"We set to work shortly after night came," Roa said. "We had to dig up the stones the terrace was paved with, which was very difficult. But after that it was easier. We started at the side of the dam away from the lake and dug a channel to the depth of a *vara*. When we came within a couple of paces of the lake we stopped. That was about midnight. We waited until near dawn, then dug again."

"A dog was barking," I said. "I wondered if it heard you."

"That was close to dawn, while we were resting. The barking we did not like. Well, as soon as we dug within a step of the lake, water pushed the rest of the dirt out and began to flow down into the plaza. In a few minutes it tore through the channel in a flood, carrying the whole center of the dam away."

"What happened in the city?"

"As Mendoza thought, everyone who could escape the torrent scrambled to the roof tops."

"And sat there while you gathered up the gold?"

"Sat, though they made gestures and yelled at us, especially the women, and threw a few stones."

"The cacique did nothing?"

"Why should he? He has gold to last a hundred years."

Roa glanced at the heavily laden train. "And so, *caballero,* have we."

At a slower pace we again set off, heading toward Háwikuh. Not long after, we learned that Indians from Tawhi were pursuing us. Tigre, who was trotting along in front of Mendoza suddenly stopped and sniffed the wind.

Mendoza pulled in his mount. The dog was facing a low ridge, not far distant, that ran parallel to the course we followed. Piñon grew there and scattered brush. As we watched, an Indian with red marks on his chest crawled from a bush and ran to hide behind a tree. A second Indian followed.

"They are beyond reach of the crossbow," Mendoza said, "and we have no powder to waste."

Roa said, "Why not pursue them, and kill a few?"

"When we camp they will come closer," Mendoza replied.

He called the dog and we set off, traveling a short distance to the mouth of a wooded ravine. Here we found a spring and a place nearby where we were protected from the rear by a steep hill. The animals were tethered on short ropes. The bags of gold we piled up, making a small fort.

No Indians were in sight, but while we ate supper Tigre stalked back and forth in front of the bulwark, stopping from time to time to sniff the air.

Mendoza tied the dog to a stake and threw water on the fire. With our weapons at hand, we waited for night and the attack we were certain would come.

217

"They will try to steal the horses," Roa said. "We should ride out and give them a scare."

"If we do so," Mendoza said, "we thereby leave the animals and gold unguarded."

He looked across the dead fire at me.

"I have my crossbow," I said.

"Good," he answered. "The gold has brought you alive. It was different, *muchacho*, before the gold."

Tigre stood at the end of the leash, the muscles under the gray coat taut, a thread of saliva hanging from his mouth. After months of harsh training, he was no longer a friendly dog, wagging his tail at every kind word, but a dangerous beast that all of us feared, save Mendoza.

Tigre suddenly growled, and peering toward the ridge, I saw at a distance of half a furlong two figures crouched behind a bush. As I stood up, an arrow sped past me, and almost at once a second struck my corselet. A bolt from Roa's crossbow hit a tree behind the two Indians, who were now running toward the ridge.

Mendoza untied the big dog. "Santiago!" he shouted.

At the command, Tigre leaped the bulwark. He overtook the first of the two Indians and, not stopping, slashed at his leg. With a cry the man went down, but the dog ran on and caught the second Indian as he reached the ridge. For a moment or two dog and man were outlined against the sky. Then I could see only the dog trotting back toward the Indian who lay writhing on the ground.

"No, Tigre," Zia cried. "No!"

The big dog must have heard her, for he halted and looked up.

"Santiago!" Mendoza shouted.

Obeying his master's command, Tigre ran on to where the Indian lay. There was a low cry, silence, then the dog came bounding back to his master.

*"Mucho macho,"* Mendoza said, patting his head.

A cool wind had sprung up out of the north. Roa wanted to rebuild the fire.

"We have killed only two Indians," Mendoza said, "there are more."

"The rest have gone," Roa said.

"They may come back," Mendoza said.

But Roa was right. We never saw the Indians of Tawhi again.

# 27

---

THE NEXT MORNING, after traveling an hour, Mendoza wanted to know if I thought there was a shorter way to Háwikuh.

"As the eagle flies," I told him. "Coming, we followed the river north, then turned west. Thus our course formed a right angle and was therefore longer by four or five days than need be." I showed him the map of a shorter route that I had made at Tawhi. "On this course, however, we may encounter rivers and mountains we cannot cross."

"God is with us," Mendoza replied, "so we travel to Háwikuh by the shortest way."

Father Francisco did not hear these words. If he had, I am certain he would not have agreed with Mendoza that God was with us. Every step we took, he would have said, was a step along the devil's own road. And this, as God is my witness, would have been the truth.

At noon I took a reading from the cross-staff, and with my notes and some guessing I plotted a straight line south-by-east to the latitude of Háwikuh. On this new course we set out, riding again in helmet and corselet.

Spring had settled on the land. Grass was fetlock deep, deeper in the swales, billowing like water blown by the wind. White-boled aspen had come into leaf, and the leaves turned on their stems like bangles. Birds larger than our hens in Ronda were everywhere, blue-colored and so tame you could pick them up.

We camped that night at the mouth of a box canyon, where a stream no wider than a man could leap tumbled down. Along it were dams, ascending the canyon like ladders, made of tangled branches and aspen trunks. An animal, which was as big as a small dog and had dark fur and a short, flat tail, lived in these dams.

Where we camped the stream fanned out into a small pond and in the clear water dozens of fish lay on the bottom, their fins gently moving. They had spotted green backs and pink sides and were fat, but we could not catch them since we lacked the necessities.

We had seen no Indians that day, yet again Mendoza had us make a fort of the bags.

As Zia and I were finishing the task, I heard the rustle of twigs and glanced up to see a deer with knobby horns standing on the far side of the pond. It looked at us curiously, drank the cold water, then stood for a while with a wet muzzle trying to catch our scent. As it moved away, Roa, who was tending the mules, picked up the matchlock and fired. The deer jumped high. It ran along the edge of the pond, and fell in the marshy grass.

Zia left me, and leaping the stream, ran to where the deer lay, its muzzle lying in the water. She pulled the body back into the grass and straightened the head and the crumpled legs, so the deer seemed not to be dead but sleeping. She then broke four small boughs from a juniper bush and laid them around the body in the four directions — North and South, East and West.

Always when a deer was killed, she did this. It was a ceremony, a sort of apology for the act of killing. It was made to the animal who was dead, in the name of the living, of the law which decreed that all life was kin, one to the other — the juniper bush, the deer, and the girl.

And always Mendoza watched the ritual with amusement. This time, however, as she stood in the meadow before the fallen deer, saying words he could not understand, he was impatient. Jumping the stream, he hurried to where the deer lay.

"Night is almost here," he said. "We have no time to waste on this business."

Zia put out a hand to fend him off, but he pushed her away, and slipped a knife from his doublet.

She raised her eyes from the deer and looked at him. "The flesh, which you eat of this animal, will lie heavy on your stomach," she warned him. "It will not nourish you nor give you strength."

"There is much work to be done," Mendoza said. "Go, young woman, and do it."

Zia knelt, and as if he were not there cutting the deer apart, went on with the ritual. Only when she was finished did she leave to help me with the bags.

"He thinks of nothing except the gold," she said. "It is a sickness."

These were the words Father Francisco used, speaking of Mendoza.

That night, though the dog Tigre was better than all of us at guarding the camp, the Captain set watches.

At dawn we were again on the trail to Háwikuh. All that day Mendoza urged the *conducta* on. It was our custom to travel two hours and rest one, for we had found that laden animals fed on grass suffer if not rested in this proportion. But he stretched our marches to two and a half hours, then to three. Riding back and forth, he kept an eye on the mules, on those that lagged, on the packs to see that they kept their balance, that no bag worked loose and was lost.

Late in the afternoon I saw far off on the horizon a misty blue shadow. It was some fifteen leagues away, a range of mountains that ran full across the horizon. I pointed it out to Captain Mendoza.

"Our course," I told him, "takes us straight into this sierra. It might be wiser to travel east or west and avoid it."

"We travel on," Mendoza said.

The next afternoon we reached a plateau which gave us a clear view of the sierras. Throughout the day, as the *conducta* toiled upwards to a plateau, we had glimpsed their snow-covered crests. But now they loomed above us, filling the horizon east and west for some twenty leagues, a wilderness of wooded canyons and stony scarps.

Nightfall was still two hours away, but there was wood about and a small stream meandered along our path, so here Mendoza ordered us to encamp. Roa went out to kill one of the numerous *antílope* that stood watching us at a distance. They proved fleet of foot, however, and he was content to bring back a plump turkey, which we fried over the coals. While we ate, Mendoza held council.

"We cannot climb the sierra with laden beasts," he said. "We must travel east or west, one or the other. Which is it, maker of maps?"

"Either way," I replied, "is off our true course."

"Which is better?"

Father Francisco spoke up. "Let us bury the gold and seek a pass through the sierra."

Mendoza gave no heed to this advice. Sooner he would have buried all of us. He spread out the map I had made of Háwikuh, the trail leading from it to the city of Tawhi, and the trail leading to Háwikuh from the Sea of Cortés. The latter trail, through Chichilticale and the Valley of Hearts and thus to the sea, seemed to interest him the more.

Turning to Roa, he said, "At dawn take the best horse and ride east. Seek out Háwikuh and there recruit four mules and two muleteers. Meanwhile, we travel west from here to where the sierra ends. Then we make a circle and turn eastward to meet you as you come from Háwikuh with mules and muleteers."

Again he studied the map, and as he did so a flock of young turkeys came to rest in a tree not far away. They huddled together on a dead branch, six in a row and, ruffling their feathers, made ready for the night.

What I thought was a seventh then flew up and perched

at the row's end, close to the trunk. I saw that the new-comer was not a turkey but a large bird, either owl or hawk. Slowly it edged along, nudging the turkeys close together, nearer to the end of the branch, until suddenly one of the birds, shoved too far, fell off. With a quick swoop the bird of prey grasped it and silently flew off.

As I sat watching this little drama, I wondered why Mendoza was so interested in the road to the sea. Was it possible that he was sending Roa to Háwikuh just to be rid of him? Was Roa the hapless fowl in the tree? When he was gone, would Mendoza turn the *conducta* toward the coast, traveling southward then to Culiacán?

With Roa left behind, Mendoza would have all the gold for himself.

# 28

IN THE MORNING Roa rode to the east and the *conducta* turned westward. For three days we traveled, slowly because the plateau was riven by many arroyos. On the fourth day, because the animals needed rest, we stayed in camp, treating their galls as best we could and gathering grass to make fresh pads for their backs.

It was on this day, toward evening, that Mendoza again called for the map. When I spread it out on the pile of bags he studied it for a long time, but said nothing.

I walked to the fire where Zia was cooking our supper. Lured by the good smell of meat which was beginning to brown, Tigre had eased up to the edge of the pit. Zia pushed him away, not far because of his size. Twice before he had snatched our meal, just as we were ready to eat.

Mendoza shouted. The dog bounded off, made a circle of the bags, playfully leaped upon them, scattering the map, then leaped down and ran back to the fire.

With a curse, Mendoza picked up a stone and threw it. The stone struck the big dog on the leg. It was a glancing blow, not really hurtful, but Tigre whirled about.

Mendoza snatched up a length of firewood and walked toward him. The dog did not move.

"*Vaya*," Mendoza shouted, raising the club.

Still Tigre did not move.

Mendoza was now only a few paces away, holding the club over his head, ready to strike or throw it. He paused as he heard the dog growl, not out of fear, for he was fearless in all things, but thinking that Tigre would obey him.

"*Vaya*," he shouted again.

Tigre stood facing his master, feet spread and teeth bared. He had the same wild look in his eyes that I had seen before on the night that he had killed the two Indians.

Mendoza threw the club with all his strength. It missed the dog, skittered along the ground and struck the fire, upsetting the meat. Tigre turned to look at the club, then for a moment at Mendoza. His eyes had grown wilder. Slowly he glided past me. I could hear the chattering of teeth and feel his hot breath upon my hand.

Mendoza took a step backward. He raised one arm to protect himself and at the same time reached for the dirk he carried strapped to his thigh.

With a swift lunge Tigre was upon him. The powerful jaws fastened upon his throat. Mendoza cried out once, as I ran for my crossbow. But by the time I had reached it and had strung the shaft, he lay quiet upon the ground and the big dog was bounding away toward a thicket.

There was nothing that we could do for our Captain.

He died without speaking to us, still grasping his dirk.

By firelight we dug a shallow grave and buried him, rolling heavy stones upon the grave against marauding beasts. Father Francisco said a prayer for his soul and we sat down by the fire. No one ate. The fire grew low. A half moon came up. From time to time the big dog howled from the thicket.

Father Francisco said, "In the morning we will dig yet another grave. This grave we will dig deeper than the first. Into it we shall put the gold and cover it well so that no man can find it, ever."

I did not answer him, thinking this is right, this is what we should do, with the first light of morning. But when the others lay down and fell asleep I rose and went to where the leather bags were piled together.

Light fell upon them from the moon. In the soft glow each bag shone forth like a block of gold, bright as the gold it held. I walked around them, counting each, changing the gold to *castellanos*. In my mind the coins took shape and stood there in rows that reached higher than my head. A duke's ransom, I thought, gained by toil, snatched from danger, at the awful cost of men's lives, to be buried in the earth and never found.

I went back and lay down by the fire. But as I closed my eyes I could still see the coins stacked one upon the other, row upon row. I slept feverishly and dreamed that I rode through the cobbled streets of Ronda, showering golden coins upon the throngs that followed me, from bags which were bottomless.

Long before dawn, with only firelight to see by, quietly

I began to load the mules. It was toilsome work, work for two men, yet soon after the sun rose the bags lay in their wooden saddles and the *conducta* was in line, ready to leave.

I went to Father Francisco. He was already awake.

"For an hour or more," he said, "I have been watching. And as I watched, I thought already he is like Mendoza, the stealthy movements, the way he takes each bag, as if it were a child he is holding."

"It is late," I said. "The sun grows hot."

"Soon, very soon, I thought, he will be Mendoza."

"By right of succession," I said, "I now command the *conducta*. Do you wish to stay with us or go to Háwikuh?"

In answer, Father Francisco hobbled off to wash at the stream. Zia, who knelt at the fire making corncakes, rose and looked at me.

"You may ride Blue Star," I said to her. When she showed no pleasure at this, I said, "Move along, the horse requires a saddle."

We broke camp and riding in Mendoza's place, I led the *conducta* toward the south.

Before we left I went to the thicket where the big dog had hidden. He lay with his head on his paws, looking out at me. I called his name but he did not move nor show by any sign that he knew my voice. I then held out a piece of deer meat, which we had not eaten. At this he growled and bared his teeth. In his eyes was the same wild look I had seen before.

I left Tigre there and mounted my horse and led the train out of camp. I thought that he might follow us, but he did not move from the thicket as we rode by. It hurt me to leave him behind, for somehow, remembering that once he had been a friendly dog, I did not blame him for Mendoza's death.

When we came to the top of the rise I glanced back. Tigre had crawled out of his lair and now stood beside Mendoza's grave, a big gray figure with head raised, looking at us as we disappeared.

# 29

OUR WAY AROUND the high sierra was through groves of aspen and flowering meadows and streams fed by melting snow. In each meadow we came to, Father Francisco stopped to gather blooms. When we reached a break in the forest, which revealed the towering peaks above us, Zia wanted to stop and make a map.

"I will get the materials," she said, "and mix the colors. This morning I scraped the pots. I have a whole bag of soot to mix."

"We have no time for maps," I said.

"A small one?"

"Neither small nor large," I said. "We have a long way to go."

On the third day at evening we overtook a small band of Indians, camped at a spring. They had come into the north, we learned, to trade parrot feathers for blue and green turquoise and were returning to their home.

The chief wished to know what we carried in the leather bags.

I warned Zia against him, but she paid no heed. Opening one of the bags, she scooped up a handful of the dust, and held it out for him to see.

The chief walked away, showing no interest in the gold, and came back proudly with two pieces of turquoise, the color of the sky.

"For the white man who has only bags of dirt." As he gave me the turquoise he glanced at the matchlock. "What?" he asked, pointing.

Like Mendoza before me, I raised the weapon, fired at a sapling tree and as it splintered pushed the smoking musket toward him. Frightened, he refused to take it.

There were three women in the camp and only four men, yet I took care to camp at a distance and tethered the stock where it could be watched.

While we were eating supper, the chief came with one of his men. They sat for a time, silent, then the chief asked about the animals. My reply to him was the same Mendoza had given the chief of Tawhi, word by word. I hoped it would have the same effect.

After the chief left, Zia went to talk to the Indian women. She was gone a long time, but came back with nothing to say of what she had heard.

"Do they have good thoughts?" I asked her. "Will our animals be safe? Ourselves? The gold? Speak, señorita. These are things of importance." I was angry at her silence, her Indian silence. "I command the conducta. I wish to know."

We were standing beside the fire. Stooping, she placed a stick of wood on the coals, and rose to face me.

"Hearing your words," she said quietly, "I think it is

232

Captain Mendoza who has come back from his grave and is talking."

"One or the other, it does not matter which." Angrily I reached out and took her by the shoulders. "Speak!" I shouted.

She pulled away and ran to the far side of the fire.

I lowered my voice, lest I rouse Father Francisco who was asleep, and softened my words. "You have heard many things tonight, Zia, talking to the women. All I wish to know is this. Are we safe from attack? Should I sit all night on guard? Or can I sleep?"

"The Indians," she said, "do not want your gold, which they laugh at and think is worthless. Nor do they wish the animals. Nor your life. Nor mine. Nor the life of anyone."

She came around the fire and stood in front of me.

"Why are you like Captain Mendoza?" she said. "Why do you think all Indians are devils? Why is there fear in your heart?"

"We shall not attack them," I said. "But will they attack us? That is all I wish to know."

Walking into the dark, she did not answer.

I wanted to believe her, but caution gained the upper hand and I made a pallet near the gold, where I could keep a watch on it and the grazing animals. Only toward dawn did I sleep and then briefly.

Without Roa and Captain Mendoza, the loading of the bags was hard, though one of the Indians helped at the task. Father Francisco again urged me to bury the gold.

"When we meet Roa," he said, "the two of you can come back and dig it up."

"The gold we do not bury," I said.

The cacique stood with the other Indians, watching the bags as they were loaded. I wondered why they followed every move I made. When we were finished I asked him the direction to Háwikuh and the distance.

"Ten suns away," he said.

"How can it be so far?" I asked.

"There are other mountains, higher than you have passed," he said. "They lie between this spring and Háwikuh. It is necessary to make a journey around them. It will take twenty suns with the burden you carry."

The Indians made ready to leave, carrying their goods on a sort of sled drawn by two small dogs. I was saddling my horse when Zia came up behind me.

"These people are from a country near my home," she said. "They now go back to that country and I go with them."

I dropped the girth, not believing what I heard. "You cannot leave," I said. "We need you."

"You need no one," she said. "You are like the other, who needed no one."

"You have been with the *conducta* for most of a year," I said.

This had no effect upon her.

"Think, Zia, of all the maps we shall make together. There are many which we have not made. In Háwikuh, we shall make them."

"You will not make them in Háwikuh," she said, "nor

in any place. Never again, because now you have the gold."

"You will miss Blue Star," I said.

"Yes, very much," she answered.

"If you do not leave, you can have her to ride. Just as you did at Tawhi."

She hesitated, looking at me and again at the colt.

"You can have the best saddle," I said, seeing her uncertainty. "The one with the hawk's bells. I will also give you a pair of spurs."

She turned away from the colt and looked up at me. "I leave now," she said.

I knew then that I could not change her mind. Untethering the colt, I handed her the halter. "She is yours," I said. "It is against Cortés' decree, but so are many things. When you reach your home in Compostela, tell your friend the alcalde that someday I will visit his city and explain why the colt is yours."

I held out my hand and boosted her to Blue Star's back. There were tears in her eyes, as she tried to speak, but I gave the colt a slap and sent them off together. For a long time, while I stood there in the grass, I could hear the tinkling of the silver bells she wore on her corncake hat.

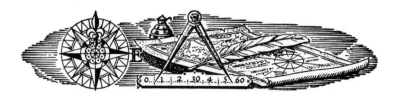

*The Fortress of San Juan de Ulúa*
*Vera Cruz, in New Spain*
*The twelfth day of October*
*The year of our Lord's birth, 1541*

TODAY THE TRIAL begins late, because the wind blows and the boat from Vera Cruz has trouble reaching the fortress. I walk the cell back and forth, a hundred times. I stop and look through the window. I walk again, up and down. It is noon before Don Felipe comes to take me away.

Today in the courtroom there are two palm fans and two boys to pull at the ropes. Still it is sweltering hot. The judges sit in their black robes, with sweat shining on their gray foreheads.

I peer everywhere through the crowded room, as I take my seat. Zia is there, so Don Felipe has told me. She has been brought within the hour from Vera Cruz. But I fail to see her.

My counsel asks me questions, which I do not remember. There are remarks by the royal fiscal to the judges. These also I do not remember. I wait, aware of little that goes on, for the moment when Zia stands before the judges and takes the oath upon the cross.

The courtroom is quiet. I hear her before she comes into my view. It is the bells, the silver bells on the corncake hat, that I hear. They sound different here in the courtroom from the time long ago when I heard them in the Land of Cíbola. Yet I cannot mistake them.

She is somewhere behind me. I turn my head. A woman, wearing the hat of Nayarit, stands against the wall, but it is not Zia. She must be making her way through the crowd, though there is no sound of her steps, only the tinkle of the small bells. While I search for her behind me, she appears from another part of the courtroom and approaches the three judges.

She stands facing them, hands at her sides, in leather jacket and skirt and red-laced leggings, with long black hair lying on her shoulders, grown up yet still a girl.

After she swears upon the cross, the royal fiscal asks, "How long were you a member of Captain Mendoza's expedition?"

"Many months," she replies.

"From the summer of '40 to the spring of '41?"

"Yes."

"In that time did Captain Mendoza find a great treasure of gold?"

"Yes."

"In the City of Tawhi?"

"There at the bottom of a lake, which the people had."

"Of what dimension was this treasure?" Zia does not understand the word "dimension." "What was the size?" he asks. "How many bags were needed to hold the treasure?"

"Many."

"And many horses and mules to carry it?"

"Yes."

"When Captain Mendoza died, who took possession of the treasure?"

I lean forward in my seat. I glance at my counsel and catch his eye. He is surprised as I am that the fiscal has passed over the death of Captain Mendoza. Has the fiscal decided to drop the charge of murder against me? Has he already learned from Zia the truth of my innocence? Is it only the gold he is concerned with — if it were really found and in what quantities?

These questions race through my mind, but it is too soon to know. The royal fiscal is cunning. He may come back to the death of Captain Mendoza later.

Zia has turned to look at me. She says nothing and the fiscal clears his throat.

"When Captain Mendoza died, who took possession of the treasure?" he asks again.

"Señor Sandoval."

"The one who sits there?" he asks, pointing at me.

"Yes, Estéban de Sandoval."

"As you know," he says slowly, "this man stands guilty of withholding a portion of the treasure, the King's Royal Fifth, which came into his hands at the death of Captain Mendoza. Furthermore, he has admitted the crime of hiding the treasure, and in a place known only to him and to you."

A falsehood. Never have I said that Zia was with me when I hid the gold. But this she does not know.

The royal fiscal fans himself with the sheaf of papers he holds in his hand, then fixes her with a friendly eye.

"You were with Estéban de Sandoval," he says, "at the time he buried the gold. You therefore know how it was buried and where. Tell the Royal Audiencia just what you saw at this time."

Zia stands calmly before the three judges. Her face is without expression. Often have I seen this look before.

"I know nothing of the thing you speak of," she says. "The gold belonged to him. To Señor Sandoval."

She pauses and once more turns to look at me. Her eyes are the color of obsidian stone, so large that I see nothing else.

"The gold belonged to Señor Sandoval, it is true," the fiscal says. "But you were there at the time it was hidden. Tell me, what did you see?"

Zia glances at the judges, at the royal fiscal.

"If he hid the gold," she answers, "I did not see it done. I know nothing more about the gold."

"You were not there?"

"No, not there."

The royal fiscal must be disappointed at this answer, but he does not show it. He asks the question again, in different words, and gets the same reply.

He looks at his papers. "Going back to the bags," he says. "To the bags carried by the mules and horses. How do you know that they were filled with gold?"

"Because I saw the gold."

"When did you see it?"

"Once when a bag fell from the pack saddle and broke open, I saw it. And when Señor Sandoval and I showed the gold to an Indian."

"What did the gold look like? Like rocks? Pebbles?"

"Not like rocks nor like pebbles. It was like salt. Fine like salt."

"And how many bags did the mules carry? Fifty? A hundred?"

"They were many bags."

"All filled with gold?"

"Yes."

Zia looks at me. It is a questioning look, as if she hopes that the truth, which she must speak, is not against me. I answer her as best I can, trying to tell her in a glance that what she has said has not harmed me with the Audiencia.

Is this all that the royal fiscal wishes to know? Nothing more? Were there in the *conducta* that left Tawhi a hundred leather bags of gold, as I have testified? Was the gold of absolute purity, not mixed with sand or tailings? Are these the questions she has been brought here to answer? I wonder, but not for long.

"The City of Tawhi," the fiscal says. "Where is it?"

"Near the Land of Cíbola," Zia answers.

"Could you find it again? Could you lead people there to see the lake whose bottom is covered with gold?"

"I could find it. But now it is bad there. Spaniards went to this city, I have heard. They went to the cliff, but could not climb to the city because the Indians of Tawhi would not let down their ladder. Also they killed all the Spaniards, eleven of them, with stones. One of the Spaniards the Indians killed was Señor Roa who was with Captain Mendoza when the gold was found."

240

I am distressed to learn of Roa's death but not surprised, for like Mendoza he feared nothing and loved gold.

"The gold at the bottom of the lake," the royal fiscal says. "Do you know where it came from?"

"The cacique of Tawhi once told us that it came from a mountain. In the city of Nexpan we heard that it came from a stream."

"Do you know this mountain or this stream?"

"There are many mountains near the City of Tawhi. I do not know the one where the gold is found. Nor do I know the stream."

"If you were to go to the City of Tawhi, if you went there with soldiers, could you find the mountain?"

"I will never go to the City of Tawhi again," Zia says. "With the soldiers or without them. Never again."

Once more the fiscal glances at his papers. He does so, I feel sure, to cover his disappointment. He has learned that the treasure exists and in a large quantity. But he has neither learned where it was mined nor, more than my notes show, where it is hidden. He has not asked about Mendoza's death, because he already knows the details of that happening.

The counsel makes a short speech in my behalf, the fiscal a long one, of which I hear little, and closes the case for the King. That is all, except for the verdict of the judges, in the trial of Estéban de Sandoval, cartographer, a native of Ronda in the province of Andalucia.

The verdict will be delivered on the morrow, or so Don Felipe tells me as we reach the terrace. I watch the crowd that comes from the courtroom, in the hope of seeing Zia before I am taken back to my cell.

She is walking through the doorway. I hear the silver bells before I see her. Her black hair shines in the sun. She walks over the stone terrace the way she walked on the trails of Cíbola, with long strides and silently.

She starts to speak, but seeing Don Felipe behind me, pauses. Then, as he moves discreetly out of hearing, she says, "I hope that my words did not harm you with the judges."

"You spoke the truth," I say, finding it difficult to say anything. "They did not ask you about Captain Mendoza's death. Why?"

"Because they asked me long before about this. They wrote a letter to the alcalde of Compostela asking. And he wrote back to them and told them what I told him, that Captain Mendoza had been killed by the dog."

It is still difficult for me to speak. It seems strange that she has come the long journey from Compostela and is standing beside me.

"The alcalde," I say, "what did he do about the colt I gave you?"

"She is mine. The alcalde made a new law for me and let me keep her, because I was with Coronado on the *jornado*. I ride her everywhere. I would have ridden to Vera Cruz if my aunt had allowed me to."

I smile at the thought of Zia riding five hundred leagues and more to Vera Cruz, but know that she could.

"Do you make maps now?" she asks.

"Not like the ones we once made together."

"I think of the maps. Someday you will make another map and I will help you mix the colors."

"Someday," I answer. "You always liked the maps. That is why you went with us from Háwikuh, because of them and the blue foal."

She looks at me as if I had become a fool.

"Not for one nor the other," she says.

"And when we made the maps no more, after Tawhi, you left me."

"I left because of something else, which I told you about. Because I hated Captain Mendoza and what he did to the Indians of Nexpan and the Cloud City. Because, when he died, you were much like him."

"Then why did you come here?"

"Because I heard, everybody heard it, that you had buried the gold. That is why I came to speak for you."

I am aware that Don Felipe is scraping his feet on the stones. Before I can answer, he has me by the arm and is leading me away.

A long night stretches before me. The candle burns well. Through the barred window the star shines over a calm sea. Now I must write down the story of Father Francisco and the journey we made together into the Inferno from which few ever return, for it is this story that has brought me here to the Fortress of San Juan de Ulúa.

# 30

E WENT SOUTHWEST that day, Father Francisco and I and the eight mules and the four horses of the gold-laden *conducta*. Zia and the Indians were in front of us, but we went so slowly that they soon disappeared from view. Late in the afternoon we came to a place where their tracks curved off to the east. Here we encamped.

I lay awake that night, thinking of what I would say to Father Francisco when morning came. For I had already made up my mind that I would not take the gold to Háwikuh.

All that day, while we had skirted the high mountains, watched the Indians grow small in the distance and at last disappear, I had thought of the gold.

If I carried it on to Háwikuh, there would be trouble. Torres would claim a share, which was not due him. Velasco, who had loaned Captain Mendoza two mules, and was known as a usurer, would claim more than his share, perhaps a fifth of the treasure. And there were others who would make claim upon it for one reason or another — the loan of powder and lead, a matchlock, a breastplate, or merely a pot to cook in.

But it was not that I feared the trouble Torres, Velasco and others would cause so much as I feared Roa. At the moment of Captain Mendoza's death, though he was away on his journey to Háwikuh, he had become the leader of the *conducta*. The treasure was therefore his.

Aware of my small part in the gathering of the gold, that I did not favor the breaching of the dam and was not even trusted to help with it, Roa would consider a bag, one small bag — if that much — ample payment for what I had done. It was not fair, I thought, that I should receive so little. I therefore had decided to take the gold to the King's officers in Culiacán, where I would have a better chance of getting my rightful share.

In the morning I rose in the dark. Working like a madman, I had packed six of the mules by the time Father Francisco awakened.

"You are in a hurry to get to Háwikuh," he said.

I said nothing, but went on loading the mules.

"Roa should be here today," Father Francisco said. "He will bring mules and men to help. Why kill yourself? We will take the day to rest and look for what we can find in the way of flowers and insects. Yesterday I came upon one that I have seen before near Jerez. A fuzzy little fellow with eight legs."

Mendoza's death gave me an extra horse, so I was able to lighten each of the loads. The sun was more than two hours high before we started off and I was so tired I could scarce mount the saddle. To Father Francisco I said nothing of my plans. Passing the place where the Indian tracks curved away, I headed the *conducta* south, for the Valley of Hearts and Culiacán.

Father Francisco lagged at the end of the line. He stumped along with his eyes turned up to the sky, watching the flight of an eagle. I waited for the moment when he would see that we were traveling not toward Háwikuh but in the opposite direction. Minutes went by. An hour. It was mid-morning, as I stopped at a stream to rest and water the animals, before he spoke.

He came up to me, holding a bag filled with flowers he had gathered along the way. Even then I wondered if he knew that we were not traveling toward Háwikuh.

"Where is it that we go with our evil burden?" he said.

"With the gold," I answered, "we go to Avipa. Then down Coronado's trail to Culiacán."

"Why?"

"Because the treasure belongs to us. Not to the leeches in Háwikuh."

He began to sort out his flowers. "The gold," he said, "belongs to the people of Tawhi."

"To Roa," I answered. "To him first. Afterwards to the rest of us."

"If the gold belongs to Roa, then give it to him. Wait here until he overtakes us and put it in his keeping."

"That means trouble in Háwikuh," I said. "Everyone will demand a share of the treasure."

"It is not your problem. It is Roa's."

I swung into the saddle. There was no point in further talk. The morning was almost gone and we had made only a league. Father Francisco went on sorting out the flowers.

"Do you go?" I said.

He glanced up at me. In his eyes was a look I shall never forget. I see it now. I shall always see it. It was a look of compassion and pity. But it was more. It was a look of fear, as if he saw my soul poised on some noisome brink.

"I go with you," he said. "With you and the devil's burden. We go together and may God go with us both."

The country was open, with no mountains that I could see. At noon I took a reading on the cross-staff, and made a slight change in our direction. We had traveled less than two leagues since morning, so riding back and forth, I urged the *conducta* along. I had a strong feeling that Roa had met the Indians and learned that we were behind them, that he would come to the place where we had curved off to the south, and follow us. Whenever we reached the crest of a hill I would look back, thinking to see him.

The country continued open and grassy. We passed through vast fields of wild flowers, yellow and blue and red, bright as the paint the Indians used. Father Francisco was beside himself with joy. He ran everywhere, plucking blooms until his sack was full.

"What do you do with all the flowers?" I asked, for some reason annoyed, though I never stopped for him and he always caught up. "What," I asked, though I knew very well.

247

"I press them between slabs of stone or wood," he answered.

"What then?"

"I put them in this."

From the sack he drew forth a book with thin, wooden covers, two spans across, which I had noticed before, but never asked about.

"That is all you do?"

"That is all I have done. But someday when I reach Culiacán or Compostela I will send a letter to my brothers in Toledo and tell them about the book and the flowers I have gathered in the Land of Cíbola."

"That should please them," I said, still annoyed.

"I hope so."

We came to a ridge from which I could look back along the way we had traveled. I saw a herd of deer grazing, but no sign of Roa. Yet I urged the *conducta* on, traveling until dark, in fear that he was somewhere behind me. If he were, and caught up with us, there would be a bitter fight, for I was determined that I should receive my share of the treasure.

# 31

N THE SIXTH DAY, having traveled some thirty leagues, as nearly as I could tell from the cross-staff, with no trace of horsemen in the country we had left, I made camp beside a stream and for a day rested the animals.

Traveling southward, we left the rolling country, thick grass, and numerous springs. On the tenth day we entered a plain that stretched away beyond the eye's reach.

We found no water here, used all that we carried, but two days later came to a brackish hole, where I watered the animals and refilled our casks. Both mules and horses needed rest, yet fearing that Roa followed us, I decided to press on and rode until late.

The morning of the fifteenth day we reached a shallow stream of mud-colored water. Thinking to throw Roa off our trail, I led the *conducta* into the stream and traveled westward for more than a league, along its many windings, leaving no tracks. I then cut back to our southward course again.

After this I lost some of my fear of being overtaken. Still, at night I never slept well and in the morning I woke uneasy.

We came upon the Inferno without warning.

At the crest of a steep rise, I saw beyond me a sink, a vast hole in the earth. It lay directly in our path, a distance of a league or more, extending east and west beyond my vision. It was a great depression in the earth, flat, naked of trees or brush, and stark white in color.

The way into it was gentle, except that the slope here was many-colored — yellow, ochre, all shades of red, and even purple. In the far distance stood a high sierra covered with snow.

"The sierra," Father Francisco said, "is like the one you see from Toledo."

He had grown weary, walking beside the *conducta*. "That one you will see again," I said to cheer him. "And when you are there once more, you will have no need to go through the streets and alleys asking for *maravedis*."

"It is not *maravedis* I will ask for," Father Francisco said. "It is for kindness and love."

I ignored his "kindness and love." "There is gold for both of us," I said.

"My share is yours," Father Francisco answered.

"There is gold also for gifts to the *Capilla de Santiago*. And for those of *Reyes Nuevos* and *San Ildefonso*."

Father Francisco was silent.

It was a windy morning and cool, but as we traveled downward the wind ceased and the sun grew hot. When we reached the bottom the air was dead and the sun even hotter than during the days in Cortés' Sea.

There seemed to be an opening to the southwest, so I set out in this direction. The earth was drifted over with a white, dustlike powder, bitter to the taste, and

250

soft underfoot. Because of the softness and the heat we made poor progress, less than four leagues from early morning until dusk, three leagues of it before we reached the Inferno.

That night I gave the animals half-rations of water and some feed from the bags, but we drank little ourselves, though our throats we dry.

We broke camp before dawn. I felt certain that by traveling hard until an hour after the sun came up we would leave the Inferno and be in open country.

The sun struck us midway to our goal — the sun beating down upon us and the burning, soft-white earth underfoot and the air so hot that it seared the lungs to breathe.

The animals began to stumble. Father Francisco, who insisted upon walking as he had on the whole journey, became partly blinded by the white, bitter dust so that he had trouble keeping up. Sighting a ledge of rocks which jutted into the sink, I led the way there, and in a thin strip of shade tethered the animals.

The shade lasted until past noon. Then we dug a pit in the soft earth and climbed in, resting there until the sun went down.

Father Francisco said, "This is the place to bury the gold. We cannot go farther with the burden."

"The burden is not one you carry," I replied. "You only need to carry yourself."

"The gold is evil," he said.

I gave the animals the rest of the water, save a little which we did not drink, and led the *conducta* out from the ledge. A waning moon cast light on the white dust. By it, moving slowly, we made another league and halted.

In an hour we moved off again, traveling until sunrise, when we passed a row of sand dunes. To their far edge, shaded from the terrible sun, I led the *conducta*. The Inferno ended about a league to the south in a grove of willows, which meant the presence of water. But we could not hope to reach the grove until after sunset, for at least two hours after nightfall.

Gazing off to the northeast, to the ridge from which we had entered the sink, I saw a flash of light. I made out a group of small objects clustered there. The flash, I was sure, came from the sun striking a breastplate. The objects were Roa, his mules and the muleteers.

Roa's mules were fresh and lightly burdened. By the next morning he would overtake us. Yet I could not move until the cool of night.

At noon the sun bore down upon us. There was no shade. A light wind sprang up, which shifted the sand around. At the edge of a dune, we again dug a hole and crawled into it. I wondered if ever we would have the strength to crawl out.

Father Francisco lay a long time without speaking. Then he said, "Here, at last, we must bury the gold."

He spoke so softly that I scarce could catch his words. I pretended that I did not hear them.

When the sun cast shade I moved the animals, staying with them because they were restless, and because I could not drive a picket into the sand and make it hold.

From time to time, through waves of heat and blowing

sand, I caught the flash of a breastplate as Roa and his band dropped down from the ridge. Far off the sun shone on the snow fields. I watched it sink, then went to rouse Father Francisco.

The hole was empty. On the bottom lay the cask, with what water there remained — a few mouthfuls. I took up the cask and shook it. The few mouthfuls were still there. Propped against the side of the pit, beside his breviary, I saw Father Francisco's book of pressed flowers.

I crawled from the pit and called his name. The wind had increased. Sand was moving everywhere, but I made out three steps towards the dunes. I followed where they led and found him lying on his back, his arms outstretched.

He breathed as I picked him up, but by the time I had staggered back to the hole and lifted the cask to his lips, he was dead.

I waited until nightfall. I had little strength left, but with it I lifted Father Francisco's body and placed it across the saddle. He was as light as a boy. With empty cask and his book of flowers, I climbed up behind him.

At midnight I reached the willows. Long before, the mules had begun to prick up their ears, so I was not surprised to find a good spring there. I laid Father Francisco on the ground. I watered the animals, drank my fill, then tethered them in tall grass, and being too weak to unload the packs, lay down and slept.

The sun awakened me. Frightened, I jumped to my feet and glanced toward the Inferno that lay behind. The white, bitter dust glittered. There was no sign of Roa.

I dug a grave in the grass beside the spring and buried Father Francisco, placing his ivory cross upon his breast. Then I walked to where the animals were tethered and looked at the bags of gold, which I had not been able to unload. As I stood there, I heard the little priest speak again, saying, "Where do we go with this evil burden?"

"Where, indeed?" I asked myself.

"The gold is evil," I heard him say. "Here, at last, we must bury it."

"It is evil," I answered. "It is the cause of your death and the guilt for your death is mine."

The sun was very hot and I went back to the spring. I sat down in the grass and closed my ears against the voice that was speaking to me. Across the stream, in their wooden saddles, were the bags of gold. I counted them and changed the gold into golden coins, but the numbers got confused in my head because the voice kept speaking. Then I realized that the voice was no longer Father Francisco's. It was my own that I heard and the words came from deep within me.

I looked back at the path the train had made in the white dust. Sand was blowing and the horizon wavered before my eyes, yet I noticed no more than a furlong away, on the very edge of the Inferno, rows of yellow craters, which I had passed in the night and not seen.

Crossing a stretch of white dust, I made my way among them. There were fifty or more, all much alike, most of them a long jump across and filled with poisonous-looking water. The green bubbles, which rose from them, gave off a sulphurous stench.

I went back, mounted my horse, and led the *conducta* out. Picking the largest of the craters, I took the nugget I had found at Nexpan and tossed it into the yellow water. I then untied the saddles and one by one I began to drop the bags into the water. They sank fast and for a long time, since the crater was deep, bubbles rose to the surface. Each bag that I dropped into the crater was like a heavy stone, which I had carried on my back and was now free of.

I led the train back to the spring and tethered the mules and all the horses save two, for Roa. I filled the cask with water, strapped Father Francisco's book to the saddle, and rode south. I rode hard all morning, until the gold and the Inferno were far behind me.

The third day I came to a wide river. Currents were strong where I stood, so I moved east for a league or more. There at a good place to cross I saw a tall tree, the only one I had passed on the journey.

Across its broad trunk, carved deep, was a message. The message read:

ALARCÓN CAME THIS FAR. THERE ARE LETTERS UNDER THE TREE.

I found no letters, though I searched, digging in a wide circle around the tree. But the message carved on its trunk I read many times before I left. I remembered it as I crossed the river and rode south to the Valley of Hearts and Culiacán. I remembered it when I told my story in that city and was put under arrest. And I remember it now as I write of it in the Fortress of San Juan de Ulúa.

Tawhi

Mendoza
killed

ABYSS

CÍBOLA

Nexpan

Hāwikuh

INFERNO

RIVER of GOOD
GUIDANCE

Chichilticale

NUEVO ESPAÑA

ISLA DE CALIFORNIA

MAR DE CORTÉS

VALLEY
OF HEARTS

MAR
DEL SUR

Culiacán

Nalvani

A MORE DETAILED MAP of SANDOVAL'S
JOURNEY to CÍBOLA

- o — o — Alarcón      x — x — Mendoza
— Coronado      xxxxxxx Sandoval

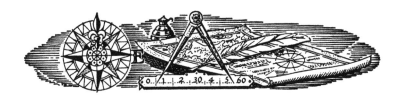

*The Fortress of San Juan de Ulúa*
*Vera Cruz, in New Spain*
*The thirteenth day of October*
*The year of our Lord's birth, 1541*

I AWAKEN EARLY, though I have written most of the night. The sky is overcast and a wind blows from the north. It has the feel of winter.

Don Felipe's Indian brings my breakfast, a large platter of *chorizos* and a mug of chocolate. I eat little but drink the chocolate, which is hot and frothy.

At mid-morning Don Felipe himself appears. He closes the iron door and stands against it, his cudgel chin thrust out. He seems to be worried about something.

"*Hidalgo,*" he says, very cheerful, which is always a bad sign with him, "you must have slept well, for you look as fresh-cheeked as a rose in the Queen's garden. Ah, to be young once more. When every day is a sweet confection to be popped into the mouth  . . ."

I wait, half-listening to this poetic outburst, until he is finished, then I ask about the verdict of the Audiencia.

"We will have word from it this afternoon," he says, "if all goes well with the judges, who are old and given to delay."

"Have you heard any news about the verdict?"

"None, but I do have news about another matter." He

takes a step towards me and lowers his voice. "Word has come to me that the royal fiscal and some of his cohorts are sending an expedition to Cíbola. They will use the notes you have given to the Audiencia. Tell me, *caballero*, will these notes lead them to the hiding place of the treasure?"

"The notes may lead there, but the treasure cannot be found."

"The map you make for me," Don Felipe says, "when will it be completed?"

"By tomorrow," I answer, "but I warn you, the gold will not be found."

"What do you mean?"

"I mean that it lies at the bottom of a deep crater. A hole, a spring if it can be called that, of burning water."

"But with the map you are making, the hole can be found? The man I send there, a trusted friend with much experience on the frontier, can go straight to this crater?"

"You do not go yourself?"

"Alas, no."

Don Felipe is embarrassed. This is the first hint I have had that he himself is a prisoner in the fortress.

"I will finish the map tomorrow," I say, "but I warn you again the gold will not be found."

"My friend will find it."

"The crater is only one of many."

"The gold shall be found."

"I have drawn everything as I remember it," I tell him. "But there are fifty or more such craters, all much alike. If I were to go there myself, I doubt that I could find it.

And having found it, I could never retrieve the gold."

Don Felipe smiles, the smile that always makes me uncomfortable. He believes that I am only trying to discourage him, that I have plans of my own to go one day and collect the treasure myself.

The iron door closes. I sit on the bench and wait. The wind grows colder and I walk up and down to keep warm, three strides one way, four strides the other. Shortly after noon, Don Felipe comes and takes me to the courtroom.

There is no sign on the faces of the judges of what the verdict will be. Wrapped in their fur-trimmed robes, they seem anxious to be done with the proceedings. Few have come to hear the verdict, but among them is Zia. She stands against the wall beside her aunt, where I can see her if I turn my head a little. Looking at her, I feel that she is more worried than I am.

The royal fiscal takes a single sheet of paper from the royal notary and begins to read, mumbling his words. He, too, seems anxious to be done with me. Perhaps, he is thinking of the expedition to Cíbola, which he will busy himself with, once the trial is over.

I hear him say, ". . . the charge of murder, in the belief of the Royal Audiencia, is unsupported by the facts and in our estimation should not have been brought. The charge of withholding the King's Fifth has been proven, and we do find the defendant, Estéban de Sandoval, guilty of that crime. We therefore sentence him, in the name of the King, His Cesarean Majesty, to five years of imprisonment."

Here the royal fiscal pauses and glances at me, thinking, perhaps, to find me shaken. I feel nothing, however, and this I show. Long before, I have steeled myself against this moment, indeed, since the day in Culiacán I confessed to the crime I had committed.

"In consideration of the defendant's youth," the royal fiscal says, "and in light of the defendant's own desire to be of help in the location of the treasure, we, the Royal Audiencia, commute this sentence to a period of three years, which is to be spent in His Majesty's prison, San Juan de Ulúa."

I look at Zia. I feel relief that my sentence is no more than it is, but her face is pale.

With a bow to the three judges, and thanking them for their courtesy to me, which Don Felipe has prompted me to do, I leave the courtroom.

I wait on the terrace for Zia. Seeing that I am determined to talk to her, Don Felipe draws away.

She is still pale.

"Three years are not long," I say to cheer her.

"Not so long as five years," she answers, "but very long. What will you do? Day after day, week after week, month after month? It is a long time, three years."

"I will do many things. And I will think of you."

The color comes back to her cheeks and she smiles her quick smile.

"Sometimes," she says, "I will also think of you. I will think of the meadow in the Valley of Hearts when we made the first map together."

"And of the time in Nexpan when you were angry with me, Zia, because I would not paint the river blue."

"Yes, I remember that day. I remember also the day when I left you, after Captain Mendoza was killed, and you gave me Blue Star."

"You were right to leave me then."

"But I would not wish to leave you again, no matter what you did."

Don Felipe, clearing his throat, comes between us and I have only the chance to say farewell before he leads me away. As we cross the terrace, I wait to hear the sound of the bells on her hat. I am almost to the stairs that lead to my cell, but I do not hear them. I turn and glance back. She is standing where I have left her. I wave and she waves back. It is then that I hear the ringing of the bells, the small, silver bells that I shall never forget.

There is little to do on the map, but while I work at it I think of the many craters, of the deep one where the gold is hidden, of its mouth yellow with crust, the sulphurous water boiling up, the bubbles that rise slowly through the slime and break, giving off their nauseous stench.

The map finished, I lift the stones and put it away. It is a good map, though not in color, everything set down — the Inferno, the soft, white dust that blinded Father Francisco, duly noted, the many craters and the spring and even Father Francisco's grave — everything as I recall it. Yet, Don Felipe will not find the treasure, nor will my notes help the royal fiscal and his expedition.

After dark, as I light the candle, Captain Martín comes to the cell. He has come by the long passage under the prison, for his doublet is dusty.

"The sentence I do not like," he says, refusing the

261

bench which I offer him. "It is too much for what you have done. Under the circumstances, you should have received your freedom. Those who have never lived on the frontier, who are ignorant of its dangers and temptations, should go there once before they die."

Captain Martín walks to the window and looks out. He turns and studies me for awhile.

"Are the notes you have given the Audiencia true?" he asks.

"Yes."

"The treasure is where you have noted it? In a place you call the Inferno?"

"Yes," I answer, surprised that he has seen my notes.

"An expedition can go there and find it?"

My surprise grows. I feel that I am listening to Don Felipe again.

"Yes, but the gold will not be found."

I tell him why, just as I have told Don Felipe. Yet, like Don Felipe, he does not believe me, thinking, once more like my jailer, that I plan to return someday to Cíbola and dig up the gold myself.

He talks quietly. "I wish to free you," he says. "Tomorrow night I have arranged for a boat to be at the landing. Your cell will be opened by a guard, not Don Felipe. You will follow him to the landing, where you will find a boat. You will be rowed across the bay to Vera Cruz. There a horse will be waiting. No expedition can start from here for another two weeks. You have the advantage of two weeks, at least, and your knowledge of Cíbola."

I am taken aback. For a moment I cannot speak. Since

he is the commander of the fortress, in charge of all prisoners, of the guards, of Don Felipe himself, his plan can be carried out. I am certain that he has thought of it in detail. I am certain, also, that he has made the offer in good faith.

I begin to speak, to thank him for his friendship and his offer of freedom, but he interrupts me.

"When the treasure is found," he says, "we will share alike. Half to you and half to me. Sixty thousand *onzas* divided is still a duke's ransom."

"The treasure cannot be found," I repeat, "by an expedition, even though the notes are truly put down. If I went to the Inferno myself and searched I could not find the crater where the gold is buried. I was exhausted when I left it there, so blinded by the sun that I scarce could see."

"Go," Captain Martín says, "and try. The guard will open your cell tomorrow night, an hour after supper."

I do not wish to tell him why I cannot accept his offer, that the burial of the gold has not absolved me of the evil nor of the wrongs I have done to myself and to others. I cannot say to him that although I am a prisoner in a fortress surrounded by the sea, whose walls are ten *varas* thick, in a cell with only one small window, still at last, at last I am free. Nor can I say to him that it is he himself who is really the prisoner, he and Don Felipe and all the rest who now dream of finding the hidden gold.

I say, "You have been kind to me, but your offer I must refuse."

He still does not believe what I have said, but at last he leaves, shaking his head.

The sea is dark and the sky clear of clouds. The star, which I should know but do not, shines in the west. In time, if Don Felipe can find me a chart, I will learn its name. If it has none, I will give it a name, in honor of the girl of the silver bells and the long black hair.

Father Francisco's book is here in my cell, hidden in the secret place. I also shall learn to know the flowers he gathered, and the many other things he found in Cíbola and loved so much. I shall read the breviary which he placed beside the cask, which was not empty when he left it there for me.

I shall give thought to the cross-staff, also. There must be some way it can be fashioned, differently from now, so that when a sight is taken upon the sun, the eyes are not blinded.

Yet three years is a long time, much longer than I pretended to Zia. I will be twenty years old when the door of my cell opens and I walk through it and up the twelve stone steps.